Damp and dishevelled, she was running, carrying her boots and trying to do her blouse up. Long locks of auburn hair were clinging to her face, and she pushed the red mane back with a brisk little gesture. She could still feel the stable lad's hands on her breasts ... she still felt the impression of his desire. As usual, ever since this spring began, she'd backed out at the last minute. Frightened at the wildness of her own response, she had torn herself away from the stable lad's arms, running towards the tall white house, wanting the safety of its solid walls around her ...

But it would not always be thus ...

By the same author

The Happy Hooker
Letters to the Happy Hooker
Xaviera!
The Best Part of a Man
Xaviera's Supersex
Xaviera Goes Wild
Xaviera Meets Marilyn Chambers (with Marilyn Chambers)
Knights in the Garden of Spain
Xaviera's Magic Mushrooms
Fiesta of the Flesh
The Inner Circle
Lucinda, My Lovely
Lucinda: Hot Nights on Xanthos

XAVIERA HOLLANDER

Madame l'Ambassadrice

Translated by Anthea Bell

GRAFTON BOOKS
A Division of the Collins Publishing Group

LONDON GLASGOW
TORONTO SYDNEY AUCKLAND

Grafton Books
A Division of the Collins Publishing Group
8 Grafton Street, London W1X 3LA

Published by Grafton Books 1983
Reprinted 1984, 1985

First published in Great Britain by
Aidan Ellis Publishing Limited 1982

ISBN 0-583-13577-3

Printed and bound in Great Britain by
Cox & Wyman Ltd, Reading

Set in Baskerville

Any resemblance to persons, living or dead, is entirely coincidental.

I

SANDRA

1

The first time Sandra de Moncet saw James Llewelyn, she had just come from the stable lad's arms.

Damp and dishevelled, she was running, carrying her boots and trying to do her blouse up. Long locks of auburn hair were clinging to her face, and she pushed the red mane back with a brisk little gesture. She could still feel the stable lad's hands on her breasts and her swollen vulva, which he had stroked for a long time – she still felt the impression of his desire. As usual, ever since this spring began, she'd backed out at the last minute. Frightened by the wildness of her own response, she had torn herself away from the stable lad's arms, running towards the tall white house, wanting the safety of its solid walls round her.

The cool grass under her bare feet soothed her. She slipped the last little round pearl button into its buttonhole, muttering to herself, 'Thursday May 24th, 1966, and Alexandra de Moncet is *still* a virgin! At this rate, my poor dear, you're never going to be another Lady Chatterley!'

Then she climbed the five steps to the verandah and ran full tilt into the man who was just coming out of the drawing room with her father.

'What on earth are you doing, Sandra?' said Adrien de Moncet.

'I'm so sorry, mademoiselle,' said the stranger, laughing. 'But I think it was your fault!'

'Sandra, you will apologize immediately. I've had quite enough of your escapades!'

'Never mind, monsieur! It doesn't matter,' the man put in. 'Are you all right, mademoiselle? I don't suppose we'll have more than a bruise or so to show for it.'

'Sandra!' said Adrien de Moncet, choking with fury.

She couldn't say anything at all. She was looking at the hands resting on her shoulders. They were warm and firm, their touch was as gentle as the silk of her blouse. The eyes looking down at hers were very dark. She saw amusement in them. And something else too – something that brought a lump to her throat. The man holding her in his arms had dark hair (one lock kept falling over his forehead), prominent cheekbones, a mouth which was rather too full, almost feminine. A face which seemed it would be ever-youthful. Sandra took all this in very fast. But all she felt was that body close to hers, which was swaying. She closed her eyes. The man's grip tightened, but the quivering of his fingers showed he was excited.

'Sandra!' thundered her father. 'I hope you are not going to pretend to be ill!'

His harsh voice, vibrating with indignation, brought her down to earth.

She drew herself up and spoke to the stranger, but her eyes were fixed on her father's, flashing fire that ought to have made de Moncet shudder. However, the former ambassador was far too experienced at reading the human face to be impressed, particularly by his own daughter.

'I . . . I apologize, monsieur,' stammered Sandra.

The hands were raised from her shoulders. She felt curiously sorry.

'My name's Llewelyn. James Llewelyn.'

He was still smiling, but there was no amusement in his eyes, only a very intense light.

'I'm delighted to meet you, Mademoiselle de Moncet.'

It was only now she noticed the slight accent which gave his voice such a vibrant, musical quality. Was he English? No, she thought American. Her mind was beginning to work again. Wasn't Llewelyn a Welsh name?

'Well, now the introductions are over, I suppose you won't mind if we get back to work, my dear James?'

Work, thought Sandra, surprised; so he's working with

Papa? How odd! He can't be much more than twenty-five.

Ever since Adrien de Moncet stopped travelling the world, six years ago, his friends had mostly been old and boring. The playboy type wasn't made welcome at the French Foreign Office in the Quai d'Orsay!

'Go away now, Sandra. Don't you have to change for tea or something? Run along, my child!'

Sandra flinched as if she had been stung. Good heavens, she thought, any moment now he'll be sending me to bed like a baby! And that man Llewelyn is smiling – laughing at me!

Furious, she turned on her heel and marched into the drawing room, first casting an indignant and imperious glance at her father.

The two men walked away towards the garden, laughing. Sandra hid behind one of the heavy, pale yellow curtains and watched them. She thought she caught a few words of their conversation.

"... still a child ... affectionate nature ... ever since her mother ..." went her father's tenor voice.

"... charming ... so young ..." replied Llewelyn's baritone.

Fuming, Sandra saw them walk off towards the poplars. What were the pair of them plotting? Her father seemed serious now. He was doing all the talking, while the other man listened attentively. Devoured by curiosity, she wondered what he was doing here – what sort of work could link him to her father? She wasn't in the least interested in politics and diplomatic intrigues, but James Llewelyn ...

'You watch out!' she said, pointing a finger into space. 'Because we'll meet again.'

And she went up to her bedroom to sulk.

Sandra paced round and round her room. With its pink and beige walls, it was a young girl's room, pretty and chaste. Adèle, Sandra's governess, had chosen the wallpaper with its pale, washed-out flowers – how she'd have liked to slap them to make them blush red! – and the cool, white, quilted bedspread, the pink satin cushions and the ruched curtains. Sometimes Sandra felt like wrecking the whole place, smashing the old vases and breaking the knick-knacks in the glass-fronted cabinet, slashing the pictures which dripped romanticism. But what good would that do? Dear Adèle, who had run the household so well ever since her mother left, would throw a fit! She'd be sure to go to Adrien, and *he* might well take it into his head to send his odd, wild daughter (looking at her, he sometimes wondered how such a strange creature could be his own flesh and blood) to see dear old Dr Blanchot! Adrien always did that when he couldn't understand her behaviour.

Sandra smiled wryly. What Adrien de Moncet didn't know was that his friend Blanchot, who put on a big psychologist act whenever he came to the house, had noticed long ago that Sandra wasn't a child any more! And he did not always act like a man of science . . .

Well, she thought, why not? Consulting Blanchot meant going to Paris, and she'd do anything to get out of stuffy old Rambouillet with its staid conventions! Why wasn't *she* allowed to go into Paris every week like her girl friends at school?

'A daughter of the de Moncet family stays at home and is never bored,' Adèle repeated whenever Sandra expressed a wish to go out with other girls, visit the cinema, do any of the things which make life bearable when you're fifteen.

Sandra just managed to stop herself snapping back at poor Adèle, 'So did my mother stay at home?'

Adèle wouldn't understand either.

Sandra's nails were digging into the curtains, but she already knew she wasn't really going to tear them to shreds. She was eager to see Llewelyn again at tea time, so this wasn't the moment to draw that kind of attention to herself. All the same, how she'd love to see Adrien's face when he looked at the wreck of her room! Just who did her father think he was? Keeper of her conscience, maybe? He did his level best to keep them from admitting that his daughter was no longer a child. He'd called her "my child" again, just now. On purpose to humiliate her! He didn't want to understand what was happening to her – or else he understood only too well.

'But I'm not a little girl any more,' Sandra whispered to her mirror, her mouth touching the cold glass.

She looked at herself critically. She liked her eyes. They were slightly slanting, and violet. An odd but interesting colour. 'You have your mother's eyes,' Adèle always told Sandra when she meant to say she was beautiful. Her nose was all right. Well, anyway it was straight, and not too long. But her chin was definitely too square, and then there was that full lower lip! Altogether, however, it was a well designed face. Those little freckles on the sides of her nose gave her an independent look. 'The face of an aristocrat,' Adèle used to say, thinking that would please Sandra.

Annoyed by the thought, Sandra took off her blouse and planted her two firm breasts with their large areolas against the mirror. She shivered as if a hand had just taken hold of the erect nipples. 'And are these breasts the breasts of an aristocrat too, Adèle dear?' she whispered. She thought of the stable lad again – but it was Llewelyn's face she saw. Stepping back from the glass, she looked at the two round marks left by her breasts. The sight was strangely exciting.

She lay down on her bed and slipped her hand under the mattress. This was where she hid the thrillers she stole from Rambouillet bookshops on days she felt brave enough – because as everyone knew, a daughter of the de Moncet family would never lower herself to read such things.

She brought out a well-thumbed copy of *The Spy Who Loved Me*. A really good James Bond, a bit more liberated than the earlier books. There was a packet of chlorophyll chewing gum slipped into it as a bookmark.

Sandra settled the cushions under her bare back and wriggled her shoulders, making herself a comfortable nest. It was very still outside, almost like a summer afternoon. She had opened the book at the page where Bond was making love to the girl narrator . . . as she read, her hand unfastened her jodhpur buttons and slipped underneath the brown whipcord. Almost at once her fingers met her rounded pubis. She wasn't wearing any briefs. Sandra read on. Her fingers thrust into her amber-coloured tuft of pubic hair and found the moist slit. Sandra moaned, her mouth open. Her forefinger and middle fingers were beginning on the familiar rhythmic movement that brought her to ecstasy.

The book dropped to the floor with a little thud which Sandra didn't hear. Lying on her back, jodhpurs pulled down to her hips – not fully developed yet but already hinting at a luscious fullness – she was in a Canadian motel with a British secret agent bending over her.

Sandra turned over on her stomach. The cotton of the bedspread rubbed against her breasts, making her shiver luxuriously. She lowered her pubis hard into the softness of the mattress. Her hand was still in place. Her bottom came up in the air, stayed there for a moment, then plunged down again. Sandra was panting. The muffled sounds she made increased her own pleasure.

She imagined a hard penis penetrating her virginal vagina.

'Wait . . . not yet . . . " she breathed. 'Wait, please . . ." And then she cried, 'Oh, James!'

She was thinking of James Bond, but it was James Llewelyn she seemed to see. She was almost coming.

The door opened.

'Sandra, you'll be late for tea!'

It was like an electrical discharge of a thousand volts! Sandra lay perfectly still. Her hand was still on her madly throbbing clitoris, and she stifled a groan of frustration and pretended to be sleeping.

'Sandra, answer me! Are you asleep?'

She does it on purpose, thought Sandra, I know she does it on purpose! She has this maddening way of never knocking! Well, I won't move.

'Sandra dear, aren't you well?' asked Adèle, worried by the girl's silence. All she could see was Sandra's back. She took a couple of steps towards the bed.

'Mm? Oh . . . is that you, Adèle? I just dropped off to sleep,' said Sandra.

The advancing footsteps stopped, and none too soon. A little closer, and Adèle was going to start wondering about this new way of wearing jodhpurs . . .

'I'll be down in a minute,' Sandra added.

Silence. Was Adèle never going to leave? Sandra felt like screaming. She ached from holding back her orgasm.

'Very well,' said Adèle. 'We'll see you downstairs.'

The door was opened as she retreated.

'And Sandra . . . you might at least be decently dressed, even in your own room!'

The door closed. Sandra let out a long breath.

She cursed Adèle. She cursed Rambouillet. She cursed herself for being only fifteen – and then she came, with a silent cry.

Sandra got ready in front of her mirror. She put on a dress with a square neckline. The hem was just above her knees; she'd taken it up herself, in secret, and was gleefully looking forward to Adèle's outraged reaction. Its apricot colour suited her. She put on her orange shoes with the little heels, and told herself that if James Llewelyn didn't gulp at the sight of her when she entered the room, she knew nothing about men. She would rather not think of her father's reaction!

Just before she left her room she put a record on her stereo. Then she ran downstairs.

When she entered the drawing room, where Adèle had served tea, the Rolling Stones were going full blast. *I Can't Get No Satisfaction* . . . Sandra's eyes were shining, and there was a little smile on her lips.

'Sit down, Sandra,' said her father calmly. 'Your tea's getting cold.'

Adèle looked at her, and then down at her cup again,

without a word.

James Llewelyn wasn't there.

Sandra could have wept – but of course, a daughter of the de Moncet family never sheds tears.

2

It was hot. Sandra looked at the thermometer on the wall of the house: the mercury was up over thirty degrees C. Lounging on the cane couch on the verandah, a glass of orange juice in her hand, she wondered what that was in degrees F, but she soon gave up trying to work it out. Too much sun. Anyway, she'd never understood conversion sums. Thinking about the temperature was only a way of trying to take her mind off James. Why hadn't he come back?

She ought to have seen him again if he was really working with her father. She supposed he was an Embassy attaché or something like that. She didn't know what an attaché actually did, but never mind! The thing was that she'd spent the last week waiting for him to come back. He had invaded her thoughts and disturbed her dreams. She almost started biting her nails again – a disgusting habit of which she'd managed to break herself – but was saved from that disaster in the nick of time by the thought that he might turn up any moment and judge her by the state of her hands.

'Don't you think you should go and do your homework, Sandra?'

Adèle had just looked out of the French window of the drawing room.

Dear old Adèle, thought Sandra, she just couldn't stand to see even a mosquito idle! To her way of thinking good girls were made to study, the way mosquitoes were made to suck their victim's blood.

However, she said, 'Yes, okay, Adèle.'

Of course, she hadn't the faintest intention of doing her homework. Her head was too full of voluptuous images, her body too heavy with its desires for her to think about work. This last week of school had been sheer torture! She sat in lessons like a robot, hearing and seeing nothing. She did not mention James to anyone, not even Lucy, whom she regarded as her best friend for lack of anyone better. James was a secret she didn't want to share. As for putting a name to the feelings that had been disturbing her all week, she categorically refused to do *that* in case they wilted like a butterfly when you touch its wings.

As Chairman of the Advisory Commission on the Development of Foreign Trade, Adrien de Moncet had set off for Paris that morning to play with his computer and bawl out a few old civil servants. Sandra had never tried to find out just what her father's resounding title really meant. All she knew was that he wasn't an ambassador any more, so she no longer went to school in Rome or Beirut. They lived all the year round in Rambouillet, which had once been their holiday home, and until last Thursday she'd felt sorry about that, and a little resentful. She was used to leading a luxurious, Bohemian life! However, May 24th had changed everything. She could almost be grateful to her father for taking early semi-retirement! She almost asked him about Llewelyn, several times, but he had been cool to her since that disastrous tea-time episode. She couldn't expect any help from Adrien – in fact, any question she asked him would only keep her farther from what she wanted to know. Or else provoke one of those frosty looks which said, 'And what in the world has that to do with you, young lady?' That was Adrien's way of dealing with awkward questions. And Sandra asked a lot of awkward questions!

'Oh, well,' she suddenly said to herself, getting to her feet. 'No more moping about. It's time I *did* something!'

And she marched resolutely indoors, to ring up every Llewelyn in the telephone book.

She met Adèle in the hall. Adèle gave her a smile, thinking she was going up to her room for a date with

Cicero. When the governess had gone off to the kitchen, Sandra went along the passage leading to her father's study, that holy of holies where no one else was allowed. Which didn't prevent Sandra from visiting it regularly, not without a delicious little shiver of apprehension. She opened the door and once again found herself in a world of paper. The walls were lined with bookshelves containing hundreds of volumes. Piles of folders stood on the heavy oak desk. To Sandra's right there was a swivelling bookcase, like a little Tower of Pisa which might topple over any moment. To her left, an open chest held a collection of back numbers of the magazine *L'Illustration*. Sandra liked this room and its special smell – a mixture of furniture polish, paper and old cigar smoke. She paused briefly in the doorway, as she did each time she invaded her father's sanctuary, then made her way towards the telephone directories piled on a pedestal table near the window. She sat down in the big leather armchair behind the desk and took the black telephone receiver off its hook with one hand, while the forefinger of the other searched feverishly for the letter L.

There were seven Llewelyns in Paris. She never even thought that James might live somewhere else. She put the receiver to her ear, mentally reciting the little speech she had prepared, and then dialled the first number.

'Yes?' said a woman's voice.

'Oh, hullo! This *is* James Llewelyn's number, isn't it?'

Someone was coming along the passage. Adrien! She hung up without waiting for the answer, and looked round for some way of escape. But the only obvious way out was by the door, and that was no good!

'There'll be trouble if he finds me in here!' she muttered between her teeth. 'Come on, my girl – think fast!'

The window? Yes, but how could she close it after her? Then she remembered the little closet next to the study, where her father kept several kilograms of extra papers. She pushed aside the big globe, which squealed as it turned on its socket, and hurried breathlessly into the tiny room. She shut herself in just as the study door opened.

She could hear men's voices, muffled by the thickness of the wooden panelling and the rows of files all round her. She recognized her father's first.

'Come in, gentlemen. We'll just pick up those notes.'

'I can't wait to hear what friend Smetlenko has to tell us!' That was a clear, young voice. Whoever the man was, he sounded cheerful.

'Quiet, Marc. You should learn to hold your tongue,' said another voice, in English. James! Sandra's pulse raced.

'Llewelyn's right. I'd rather not discuss the subject within these walls,' said Adrien de Moncet. 'Let's go out in the garden – trees have no ears.'

'He's here – he's here!' hummed Sandra as the three men left the room. When all was quiet again she extricated herself from her hiding place and hurried to her room, covered with cobwebs. A plan was forming in her head.

Sandra had put on her tennis things. Racket in hand, she looked in on Adèle, who was busy in the butler's pantry.

'I've done my homework,' she informed her. 'I'm going to play a set of tennis before tea.'

Adèle smiled at her absent-mindedly. She vaguely felt that Sandra had done her Latin translation rather fast – but the tennis club was not far from the house, and only the cream of Rambouillet society patronized it.

Sandra took care to slam the front door, but instead of making for the garden gate she went round the house to get to the out-buildings.

She stopped outside the garage and looked round. Her eyes came to rest on the arbour to the right of the verandah. Yes, there were her father and the two young men immersed in their papers, so that was all right! Silently, Sandra entered the garage by its side door from the garden. She could make out the familiar shape of her father's Rover in the dim light. Neatly parked beside the black Rover stood a metallic gray BMW with a Diplomatic Corps plate, waiting for its owner.

'That must be his,' Sandra told herself.

She went to the far end of the big, concrete-floored garage. Yes, there was what she wanted, behind that pile of tyres! She went over to the stable lad's rusty black Solex and put her racket on the carrier. Then she pushed the saddle back and took hold of the handlebars. She felt something resist her – the anti-theft device. Calmly, Sandra went back to the other end of the garage and found a pair of cutting pliers in a metal toolbox. She had seen the gardener use them to cut a railing.

A little pressure on the pliers, and the rubber-shod metal ring fell to the floor. Sandra straightened up, put the pliers down on the old tyres, and wheeled the Solex backwards again. She could get it out of its corner now.

She hadn't heard him arrive, but all the same, there he was! Staring blankly at her.

'What are you doing here?' she said.

'*I* could ask *you* that, mademoiselle!' said the stable lad. 'That's my Solex!'

'Look, I need it – I'll bring it back straight away. Let me by!' Sandra ordered.

The lad had planted himself in front of the machine. He didn't look as if he had any intention of getting out of the way.

'Hey, you've cut the anti-theft device too! Sandra, I'd have lent you the bike if you'd asked . . ."

The lad's voice was hoarse. He had that look in his eyes which could still turn her to jelly until a few days ago. Now, Sandra didn't feel the least desire for the stable lad – but he could ruin everything, and she didn't have much time to spare.

She tried coaxing. 'Listen, it's only for a bit of a run! I didn't want to disturb you. I'd have bought you another anti-theft device.'

But he had already grabbed her arm and pulled her towards him. His hot mouth was searching for Sandra's cool lips. 'Why didn't you come back?' he murmured hoarsely. 'I've been waiting for you – I want you!'

Sandra felt her defences weaken. Her body was responding in spite of herself, pressing against the stable lad's. He embraced her passionately. His hands slipped underneath her white tennis skirt and felt her rounded buttocks. Sandra stifled a moan and tried to keep in control of herself.

'I'll come tomorrow!' she promised. 'But you *must* let me go now! I'm in a hurry!'

The stable lad did not let her go. His hand was making its way up between Sandra's thighs. His breathing came faster now, and she could feel his hard penis through the thin material of her skirt.

'Okay, then – tomorrow. But if you want me to let you go –' (he took Sandra's hand and drew it down towards his penis) 'stroke me!'

Sandra bit her lips. The sensation of the stable lad's penis against the palm of her own hand excited her more than she liked to admit. But James could be getting out of his chair and saying goodbye to her father at this very moment.

The stable lad had undone his trousers. He guided Sandra's hand up and down his erection in a slow rhythmic movement, in time to his panting breath. His head buried in the hollow of Sandra's shoulder, he abandoned himself to pleasure. Sandra felt he was on the point of coming.

'No!' she said brusquely, trying to pull her hand away. 'Not here! Papa has visitors – they'll be coming to get their car.'

But her sudden movement had brought the stable lad to climax – his whole body seemed to buck as he came.

Her cheeks crimson, Sandra wrenched herself free. She grabbed the handlebars of the Solex and pushed it through the sliding door, which grated slightly. Without looking back, she crossed the gravel sweep. She hardly heard the lad call after her, 'Come back this evening!'

She went through the big garden gate, hoping no one in the house had noticed her. Then she was out on the road which skirted the property – the Paris road. Another road, lined with chestnuts, turned off it to the left. Sandra took up her position at the corner and concentrated on breathing slowly, to calm the beating of her heart.

She wanted to forget all about the last few minutes and not think of anything but James.

That's the way he'll have to come out, she told herself, and added, out loud, 'And it'll be up to me then – you'll just *have* to stop and take notice of me, James Llewelyn!'

She savoured the four syllables of his name, rolling them around her mouth and repeating them until her pulse was regular again.

The long wait began. She picked a chestnut leaf and amused herself by making it into a skeleton, carefully removing the leafy parts with the nail of her middle finger, without breaking the veins.

She wasn't going to keep that date with the stable lad. Ever! Her whole being reached out towards the man who would soon drive along the road.

But suppose, she suddenly wondered, suppose he isn't going to Paris? No, that's not possible. He *must* live in Paris!

However, she was not entirely reassured. The waiting strained her nerves. Fifteen skeleton leaves were piled up at her feet and she was just about to start on a sixteenth, when she heard the sound of an engine.

At last!

She straddled the Solex and took off with a brisk little push.

A metallic grey BMW swept past her.

Like a prima ballerina carefully timing her entrance, Sandra turned left and shot down the Rue des Alouettes, which dropped steeply to the Paris road.

The wind swept through her hair. Her eyes were shining, and a radiant smile lit up her face. Her short skirt rose in the air.

A pale young girl on a black Solex, she thought: it'd make a good song title!

She had forgotten all about the stable lad.

She stopped at the bottom of the slope, but kept the engine running. The roads in this part of town were deserted at this time of day. The good folk of Rambouillet were taking a siesta, or playing bridge or tennis – or games of other kinds behind their closed shutters. Sandra quietly settled down to wait again. He can't know the Paris road goes round in that big bend, she thought; he can't know about the short cut down the Rue des Alouettes.

Three minutes later, a grey car appeared on her right.

Done it, thought Sandra jubilantly. James, here I come!

The BMW slowed down as it approached the crossing. Mounted on her Solex, Sandra was counting the seconds. She started off at the last possible moment.

Car tyres squealed on the tarmac. 'Watch out!' someone shouted.

Looking straight ahead of her, Sandra began riding across the road. The car was almost on top of her. She braked gently, to control the shock, and the BMW's right wing hit the back wheel of the Solex. Sandra was lifted right off the machine. She sailed through the air for a fraction of a second, glimpsing the bike as it reared up, before her body came down again. She lay sprawled on the bonnet of the car. Just before she closed her eyes she saw Llewelyn's face. It was astonishingly pale.

The car doors slammed. Sandra felt a hand on her leg, and another hand being slipped under her back.

'Mademoiselle – mademoiselle, are you all right?' breathed the now familiar voice.

Eyes still closed, Sandra did a perfect imitation of a groan of pain. She'd happily have risked a broken leg to find herself in James Llewelyn's arms!

A face was bending over hers. Was that his breath warming her cheek – almost like a kiss? Through half-closed lashes she saw the alarm in his dark eyes.

'My God, it's Sandra! Sandra de Moncet!' cried the young man. 'Here, Marc – come and help me, quick!'

Marc? O no! What a fool she'd been! How *could* she have

left that possibility out of her calculations? The other man was with him! So much for her romantic tête-a-tête with James!

Arms lifted her and laid her down on the seats of the car.

She'd better get out of this fix as fast as she could! Scrapping her act as a severely injured accident victim, she opened her eyes. She couldn't help smiling at the two men's anxious faces.

'Well, mademoiselle, you can certainly boast of putting the fear of God into us! Anything broken?'

Sandra was face to face with the other man – the one called Marc. He was as fair as James was dark, and he had two dimples which somehow didn't sweeten his rather sour smile. His sharp, slightly ironic glance took in her exposed thighs and travelled up to her breasts. He was undressing her with his eyes.

'Well, I must say – what a treasure Adrien's been keeping from us!'

'There's nothing the matter with me. Let me up!' she snapped. And turning to Llewelyn, she added, 'Would you take me home, James?'

Adèle was buzzing about like a flustered bee.

'My goodness, Sandra, what on earth were you thinking of, borrowing that Solex? You know very well your father's always forbidden it!'

'It was so hot. I didn't want to walk all the way to the tennis club,' muttered the girl. She was lying on the sofa in the drawing room.

'Here, drink this. It's cognac – it'll make you feel better.'

'I don't want it. Oh, do go away, Adèle! I'm fine.'

'Show me your elbow,' said the governess. 'Are you bleeding?'

'It's only a bruise.'

Sandra freed her arm and pushed away Adèle, who looked like an offended nursemaid.

Adrien de Moncet came into the drawing room followed by the two young men. 'Well," he began, 'it's all been dealt with, so now let's forget this unfortunate accident.'

Sandra opened her mouth to speak, but her father gave her no time. She wasn't going to escape a sermon on this occasion.

'The Solex is a write-off. I shall compensate the stable lad, of course. But I don't want to see a two-wheeled vehicle in this place again.'

James Llewelyn, standing behind de Moncet, never took his eyes off Sandra. He smiled at her, and suddenly the sermon didn't matter any more. His companion, standing in the background, didn't miss that silent exchange of glances.

'Well, you're lucky that M. Renan is willing to say no more about it,' Adrien went on. 'The wing of his car is badly dented.'

'You mean it wasn't even your car?' cried Sandra, sitting up.

Llewelyn gave her an odd glance. A shadow passed over his face. The he took her hand, laughed warmly, and said, 'No, it wasn't my car, Sandra.'

Adrien de Moncet bit back the sharp remark on the tip of his tongue, and turning to Adèle, signalling to her to serve tea.

Sandra felt a burning sensation in the palm of her hand, like an electric current running through her from head to foot. Her father was not looking at her any more, so she could give herself up fully to this brief moment of happiness. Nothing would make her change her mind now! James Llewelyn was going to be her first lover!

'If I may offer some advice, Mademoiselle de Moncet,' Marc Renan remarked, 'next time you feel like playing Juliet do try to pick the right Romeo! I don't have an unlimited supply of BMWs.'

His face wore a mocking little smile.

She knew he had seen right through her.

3

Two months had passed already! As she unpacked her case, Sandra went back over all the new sensations and discoveries that had filled her life these last eight weeks. James and Marc – Marc and James! Like the two heads of a hydra. She had been sorry to leave them for her usual August holiday at Juan-les-Pins, but all the same, it was good to find herself in the big, cool, white villa again. Everything in the place, even the stone of the walls, held the imprint of her mother.

She felt happy in this bright, simple house, decorated by Anna de Moncet in resolutely modern style. The comfortable, up-to-date furniture was in complete contrast with the furnishings of Rambouillet, and so was the garden, wild with honeysuckle and magnolias. There was an atmosphere of freedom.

'Freedom!' shouted Sandra, flinging open her bedroom window, which looked out on the promenade and on the sea, beyond the pine and palm trees.

Goodbye, Rambouillet and its people! Goodbye, Crepau the bookseller, who knew she was pinching books but was scared to accuse a girl from such a blue-blooded family. Goodbye Androuet and Barbeau, the two local lawyers who came to pay their respects with the regularity of clockwork. Goodbye, girls of Rambouillet with your prim ringlets, and pimply youths with glasses! Goodbye to the local priest and the de Moncet pew in church, where one seat had been empty for the last five years. Goodbye to the interminable litanies on Sundays! Sandra was not going to think of anything but the thirty days which stretched ahead of her, like an oasis in her arid life.

She towelled her hair, which was still wet. She hadn't been able to resist going into the sea the minute she arrived. She was just taking off her bikini top to put on a T-shirt when Adèle, who would be her only chaperon for the whole month, knocked and came in.

'Well, well! Learning to knock at last, are you, Adèle?'

'Sandra, please keep a civil tongue in your head! And get dressed. Your uncle has just arrived.'

'Gregory – here already? Oh, that's marvellous!'

She hurried past Adèle on her way to the blue and white drawing room.

'Sandra, just look at you . . . !'

But Sandra wasn't listening – she was running down the stairs to the drawing room below, where a tall man dressed in white was waiting for her, arms spread wide.

'Gregory!' She flung her arms round his neck and kissed him with enthusiasm. 'How did you know I was here?'

'Take it easy, little Tsarina – you'll knock me over!' replied the man, smiling.

He had silver hair and a naturally authoritative manner. To Sandra, he was a magician. He had brought her back the nickname of Tsarina from Russia, and she loved it. It was like a secret code between the two of them – a signal of recognition.

'I have my spies!' he added, catching his niece up and whirling her about the room.

She laughed. Happy pictures from her childhood came back to her. Gregory taking her to the circus for the first time and then imitating the clowns' act in the car taking them back to Rambouillet. Gregory falling over his skis while trying to teach her to do a plough turn, and starting a tremendous snowball fight to get his revenge on her for her helpless peals of laughter! Gregory again, giving her the wheel of his Jaguar right in the middle of Paris because she'd said she wanted to learn to drive, and then trying to explain to the traffic cop that he'd felt unwell, and his niece had done her best to stop the car, and after all, those bollards in the middle of the road which she had just hit were of no real use for anything, were they? It seemed to her that most of the high spots of her childhood – those special moments that linger in the memory – were nothing to do with her parents and the exotic countries she had visited with them: she owed them to this uncle who surfaced in her life whenever things seemed difficult.

Adèle had joined them and was watching their reunion like a dachshund whose bone has just been stolen by the big Newfoundland next door. Gregory Aladin's brows drew together, and he put his niece down on the floor.

Suddenly sobering down again, Sandra cast her uncle an imploring glance. He winked.

'Come on, I'll buy you a waffle. You'd like that, wouldn't you?'

'Wouldn't I just!' said Sandra, making straight for the front door.

Gregory shrugged his shoulders slightly, with a glance at the governess. 'We'll be back soon, Adèle,' he said, before following the girl.

Arm in arm, they made for the little kiosk selling waffles on the sea front. At three in the afternoon the beach was full of bathers. Somewhere, a transistor was playing an English rock group's latest hit.

"*. . . and when I'm with you I can't control myself . . .*" hummed Sandra, in English.

'Well, well, Tsarina – your English has come on a lot since we last met!'

'Oh, I've had a good teacher! An American . . . but tell me about yourself, Gregory! Still in big business?'

'Very much so! In Hong Kong today, tomorrow in New York – I re-fashion the world to my liking!'

A momentary glow of admiration mingled with envy came into Sandra's eyes.

'And – how about Mother?'

Her tone was carefully casual.

Suddenly Aladin sobered. 'Still nothing. No news at all.'

'Oh,' was all Sandra said.

'You know I'd have sent you word if there'd been any news, Sandra. And you remember what your mother's like – whimsical, unpredictable! If she isn't keeping in touch with her daughter, I don't see why she should take the trouble to phone or write to her brother.'

'Oh, there's the waffle man,' cried Sandra. 'Looks as if we'll have to fight our way through the crowd to get at his waffles!' she added, glad to have a change of subject.

A number of noisy adolescents were clustering round the wooden hut. The youths were bronzed and very sure of themselves. A comb, a packet of Gauloises and a Zeppo lighter stuck out of each pair of bathing trunks.

'Wait here for me, Sandra,' said Gregory, in the tones of a man used to command. 'Do you still like your waffles with cream and lots of sugar?'

'Yes, Gregory – but I'll go!'

And with a self-confident air, she left her uncle standing there on the pavement. She made boldly for the counter. Her nostrils were quivering. She wore no bra, and her breasts swayed gently under the white cotton of her T-shirt. The eyes of the youths were drawn to her long legs swinging gracefully as she approached.

'Hey, look! Get an eyeful of that!' said a tall, blond boy chewing gum. He nudged his neighbour.

'Yeah – she's quite something!' replied his friend, smoothing down a few hairs which did duty as a moustache.

Imperturbably, Sandra walked on – a lamb among a pack of wolves. Some of them let out low whistles, others were devouring her with their eyes. They all stepped aside to let her pass.

'Two waffles,' she said. 'With cream and sugar.'

'Yes, mademoiselle, at once!' replied the Italian waffle seller, with a smile.

He spread the hot waffles with whipped cream and then handed them over, wrapped in white paper. The circle had closed again behind Sandra. The boys were murmuring. An arm touched hers. She felt their eyes boring into her back, and turning around, tossed back her mane of red hair. Regally, she swept the boys aside with a glance and came back in triumph to deposit a waffle in her uncle's hands. A chorus of whistles rose behind her. Sandra suppressed a smile.

'And where did you learn *that* sort of self-confidence?' asked Gregory, thoughtfully looking her up and down.

'Oh, it's the sea air, dear uncle!' she said, nose daubed with whipped cream.

But Gregory Aladin was no longer in a joking mood. He was looking at Sandra as if seeing her for the very first time.

'Enjoy yourself, and tell your uncle not to bring you home too late. Remember that a daughter of the de Moncet family . . .

'Oh, please, Adèle – *not* this evening.'

For the last time, Sandra checked her appearance in the hall mirror. Her white silk dress was just the right length – the length that made Adèle shudder! The slit up one side revealed a smooth thigh gilded by four days on the beach. Her long legs ended in open-toed white court shoes which she was wearing for the first time. The tumbling ringlets of her mass of auburn hair emphasized the romantic yet also depraved look which set her apart from other young girls.

Satisfied with her reflection, Sandra left the villa and went to the white-painted garden gate. Adèle followed, and watched her get into the big Jaguar driven by Gregory Aladin's chauffeur. It started off with a low purr. Adèle did not go back into the big, empty house until the car's rear lights had disappeared along the sea front.

Perched on one of the deep, fawn leather seats, Sandra was quivering with anticipation. This was the first time her uncle had ever invited her to one of the parties he gave regularly on his yacht, the *Rosebud*. And she told herself that the incident of the waffles had something to do with his sudden decision. As the car drove towards the harbour, she found herself wishing Gregory was her father. Then she wouldn't have had to live at Rambouillet, or go away on holiday leaving James . . . the thought of James made her shiver, and with a little animal's instinct for self-preservation she made herself banish it. This evening she took her first steps as an adult – and something told her it was a lonely game to play.

By the time the Jaguar drew up at the harbour, Sandra was ready to face the world. The chauffeur came round to open the door for her and escort her to the little white motor boat moored to the quayside. A sailor, silent and anonymous, helped her in, and the boat left the shore. Sandra sat back on the wooden seat. She breathed in the fragrance of the night and the sea, and closed her eyes, the better to hear the surge of the water, which the boat's motor could not drown. The warm wind bore the sound of music to her. The shape of the *Rosebud*, lit up like a Christmas tree, stood straight ahead. The band was playing swing music. The sounds of the party were like fragile bubbles breaking against her ear.

The boat drew up beside the ship's ladder. She saw several Chinese lanterns hanging from the rails. Now the noise was all around her, glasses clinking against a background of voices. A man in a white dinner jacket was waiting for her at the top of the ladder. The light of the lanterns played over her uncle's face, making his dark eyes glow. Like her own, they slanted slightly. For a split second she seemed to be looking at a strange captain out of some Oriental fairy tale as Gregory Aladin gave her his hand and helped her up on board.

'Good evening, Tsarina.'

'Good evening, Gregory.'

They exchanged a conspiratorial smile. Gregory gave her a glass of champagne, and then led her into the middle of the human whirlpool. He introduced her to his guests, an odd mixture of businessmen, playboys and artists, murmuring information about their names and jobs and a few acid comments into her ear, as if pouring pearls into the palm of her white hand. She got an impression of men with heavy-eyed faces and nervous hands, of the figures of elegant women glittering with jewels. She remembered only one of the names: May Campbell, a tall, dark, voluptuous woman who reminded her of Ava Gardner. She knew that May was her uncle's mistress. While Gregory was detained by a group of exuberant guests, May took Sandra's arm. They both leaned back against the side of the cabin. Intoxicated with all these new sensations, Sandra took little gulps of air. A smell of fresh paint, salt and rope mingled with the perfumes of the elegant women thronging the deck. Sipping champagne, May glanced at the girl. She had taken to Sandra at first sight, liking her look of being a little lioness crossed with a gazelle: a subtle mixture of strength and tenderness.

'Gregory's told me so much about you! I feel as if I'd known you for ever, Mlle de Moncet,' she said, and then added, 'Oh no, why should we be on such formal terms? I'd like to call you Sandra – may I?'

'Of course!' said Sandra, and they drank to their new friendship.

'Look, Sandra – none of the men have eyes for anyone but you!' May murmured wickedly. 'See that fat man with the monocle? He's been staring at you ever since you arrived.'

A corpulent man who looked ill at ease in his dinner jacket staggered towards the two women. He had hiccups, and whenever he hiccuped his monocle fell out. He kept earnestly putting it back in place. He stopped in front of Sandra, swayed about for a moment, and then said abruptly, 'Mademoiselle, this one is a waltz!'

And giving her no opportunity to protest, he took her by the waist and led her on to the shining dance floor. Sandra found herself clutched against his soft belly. One damp hand clung to her arm, another was making its way down her back. She felt as if she were choking. Alcohol-laden breath floated to her own nostrils.

'You dance well!' he said. He had a guttural accent.

'How on earth can you tell?' inquired Sandra drily. 'We're not moving – just swaying back and forth on the spot!'

Brought down to earth from his alcoholic haze, the man let go of her for a second, leaning back to adjust his monocle. He seemed offended.

This was the moment May chose to slip between the two dancers. Sandra stepped back.

'But the waltz isn't over!' her partner protested.

May had planted herself firmly in front of him. 'It is so far as you're concerned, M. Pigon! Someone else is waiting for this lady.'

'But – but . . . "

'Do you want to dance, M. Pigon? Very well, you can dance with me!'

Towering a head or more above him, May put her arms round the fat man and sketched a dance step sideways. As the dumbfounded M. Pigon fell into the rhythm she was imposing on him, May smiled at Sandra, whose eyes were shining with gratitude.

Free to amuse herself again, Sandra wandered among the guests, and danced rather listlessly with several talkative young men.

'I have a feeling you're not enjoying yourself very much, Tsarina!'

Gregory had come to lean on the rail beside Sandra. Looking out to sea, she tried to lie.

'Oh yes, I am, Gregory! I've had a little too much to drink, that's all. I don't want to have my head going round and round.'

Her uncle put an arm round her shoulders. She loved him so much, and she didn't want to hurt him – but she knew that whatever it was she was looking for, it wasn't here.

'Never mind about sparing my feelings, Sandra!' said Gregory. 'These people aren't really close friends of mine. You know . . . '

But he was interrupted by sudden bursts of laughter from

below decks. Four dishevelled young men were trying to climb the steps leading up from the saloon. Two of them were carrying a blonde, icily beautiful girl on their shoulders, while she distributed kisses of encouragement.

'Well, *some* of us seem to be having a good time!' Gregory murmured into his neice's ear.

However, Sandra just stood rooted to the spot. She thought her heart missed several beats. She had recognized one of the young men! He was putting the girl down now, and bowed to her, kissing her hand with mock solemnity. Then they both went off towards the bar at the other end of the yacht. What was he doing here? Was he a friend of her uncle's? And that woman – who was *she?* Tears of rage came into Sandra's eyes.

Puzzled, Gregory stared at her. He was about to ask what the matter was when she spoke. 'Do you know that man?'

'No, one of my guests must have brought him. But – '

The question died on Aladin's lips. Sandra was wiping tears away, and he could tell she was edgy and nervous. He held his tongue.

Sandra watched the rest of the party emerging from the saloon. Marc Renan, bringing up the rear, emptied the glass he was holding in a single draught. So they were *both* here!

'Gregory, listen. Do you think it's possible to love two people at the same time?'

Sandra's face wore such an intense expression that Aladin thought better of the light-hearted answer he was about to make. He felt there was something serious behind that naïve question. He knew Sandra had always been honest with him, and in many ways he was her confidant. Perhaps that was why Adrien had never liked him – that, and the fact that members of the de Moncet family went into the army, the Church or the diplomatic service, or at a pinch into medicine (the aristocracy's grudging concession to modern life). But never into business! His former brother-in-law had always considered Gregory an outsider and a black sheep.

The band had begun a languorous slow foxtrot, but Aladin was not listening to it. He looked gravely into his niece's eyes, saying goodbye to the Sandra he had known: a wild, affectionate little girl, amusing and obstinate. Sandra was not a child now, and he must be honest with her.

'Yes, Tsarina, it *is* possible to love two people at once.'

'Thank you, Gregory.'

Suddenly, there was Marc in front of her.

'Sandra! You – here? This is too good to be true!' He took her hands, touching her cheek with a finger that shook slightly. 'But how . . . ?'

'As it happens, Marc, this is my uncle's yacht!' said Sandra, with light irony. 'How are you? Let me introduce my uncle – Gregory Aladin.'

Marc abruptly drew himself up and tried to straighten his tie and tidy his hair. Aladin smiled indulgently.

'Don't worry, young man – you're here to enjoy yourself. And as you two look as though you knew each other pretty well, I'll leave my niece in your hands!'

He turned away, leaving the two young people face to face.

'I tell you what, Sandra – I'm going to kidnap you!' said Marc. 'Don't bother to protest. I know you won't really mind.'

'Marc, what are you and James doing at this party?'

She was looking intently at him, her expression still reserved, though her mouth was trembling, undecided. Marc's suggestion was no more surprising than his presence here! Was it such a small world that wherever she went she was bound to see these two men turn up, bringing her most intimate dreams and desires to life again? She felt as if she were the innocent victim of some plot – but at the same time a profound, quiet joy welled up from deep inside her.

'James got his friend Annabelle to invite us. She lives in Juan-les-Pins – we arrived here this evening.'

He tried to draw her towards him, but she held back. There were too many things he still had not cleared up.

'This friend of his,' she began. 'Is that the blonde I saw him carrying?'

'That's right. A remarkable girl, Annabelle.'

He put an arm round her waist, and she let him, enjoying the happiness of the moment. To hell with questions!

'Come on, then!' she said. 'Let's get off the yacht – all these people are so starchy.'

'How about James?'

'We'll go and find him.'

They found him up at the bow of the boat,
the bar that had been set up on a long table. Waiters in white were bustling around it.

'Hullo, James,' said Sandra.

There was the sound of a glass breaking. James looked down at the puddle of liquid spreading at his feet, and then up again at Sandra, whose red-gold hair shone against the night sky.

She took a couple of steps towards him, and he kissed her scented cheek.

'Let's go,' was all he said.

In the bows of the *Rosebud* a white figure leaning on the rail watched the motor boat set off, and smiled.

* * *

They had been driving about for two hours, up and down the coast, stopping at every bar that was still open to embrace each other between mouthfuls of champagne. Sitting between the two men in the front of the little Triumph, Sandra felt as if she had come to the end of a long journey at last. Yesterday didn't matter any more. Too happy to wonder about so many coincidences, she gave silent thanks to her uncle Gregory – her very own magician.

An old woman selling roses by the harbour at Antibes gave one to Sandra.

'Anyone can see you're in luck, little lady!' she said in a hoarse voice. 'Two handsome gentlemen all to yourself! Mind you keep an eye on them so they don't fly away!'

Sandra put the rose in her hair, and the Triumph set off again. They did not talk much; they were happy just to be together, and as if by common consent, they stopped at a deserted beach. Sandra lay on the sand between the two men. Her body seemed to absorb their energies. She had to make an effort to think at all, telling herself she wanted to remember this moment, treasure it in her mind for ever. James was playing with her auburn hair, Marc was holding her hand. It was as if the two men, even though they were nearly thirty and experienced in all the games of love, were waiting for *her* to give a signal.

'Why don't we bathe?' said Sandra.

She rose slowly to her feet and unveiled her body to them, offering them the sight of her nakedness. For a moment the two men forgot they were rivals and that each wanted to be the first to possess her. Then Sandra ran towards the dark sea. Marc and James undressed too.

'Coming in?' cried Sandra. 'Last into the water will never have me!'

They ran in, splashing her, and all three naked bodies touched. A last, childish fear made Sandra delay the moment when these two men would make a woman of her. They played among the breakers, gently caressing her, hot with desire. Mouth to mouth, lips to flesh, they all three came ashore in the surf, entwined together. They went back to the sandy beach. Sandra sat there at the water's edge, Marc and James kneeling in front of her. Slowly, she put her arms round their necks, drew their heads towards her own and murmured into the warmth of their throats, 'Oh, how I love you both . . .'

James took possession of her mouth. Marc was stroking her breasts. Two masculine bodies moving like one, tumbling her on the beach, their mouths caressing her skin. 'Love me!' she kept saying ecstatically. 'Oh, love me . . .'

One mouth found its way downwards to her fleece of auburn hair. She trembled, and parted her thighs. With his tongue, James opened up a way towards Sandra's vulva, licking its salty lips, plunging into the damp, throbbing warmth of her flesh.

Engorged with desire, Sandra swung her head from side to side, murmuring, 'Take me – I want both of you, both of you . . ."

The same hoarse cry escaped both men at once. Their penises, already erect, were aching – they wanted this girl as they had never wanted a woman before!

Marc pressed his erection to Sandra's full lips, and her mouth opened to receive it. She kissed the distended penis, caressed it with her tongue, almost swallowed it. Marc closed his eyes and gave himself up to her caresses, while Sandra herself undulated under the touch of James's mouth. Her whole being throbbing with sexuality, she moaned gently and uttered a first cry of release.

With instinctive harmony, the two men lowered themselves one each side of Sandra.

'I'm going to take you now,' breathed James.

'And so am I," said Marc.

'Don't be frightened – I won't hurt you.'

'Open your legs. I'll be gentle.'

'See how hard we are, and it's all yours . . .'

'I'm coming in – gently.'

'Yes – yes, come!' gasped Sandra.

James's hands were tangled in her damp bush of hair. Marc's were parting the two white spheres of her buttocks, sliding down the groove between them. Slowly, both men penetrated her. She bore the momentary pain and surprise, fascinated by the discovery of her own body she made as the two penises slowly filled her up. She opened her eyes – she wanted to see them. Her auburn hair lay spreading on the sand. Was she frightened? Did it hurt? She felt the penises plunge deep inside her, moving like living things. Then her head fell back and she wept with happiness. She cried without restraint for a long time. Her sobs mingled with the two men's spasms as they lost control, beginning to come in Sandra's sprawled body.

Suddenly it arched up under their assault.

'I'm a woman now – I'm coming – now!'

Deep inside Sandra, Marc and James climaxed, blood and sperm mingling.

Minutes passed before they moved again. Then they went back into the cool sea.

'I want to sleep with you – both of you,' said Sandra.

'What about Adèle?' asked James.

'Oh, never mind Adèle! Take me back with you.'

Annabelle's villa was pleasantly cool. James and Marc knew its owner would not be back that evening, and they went on exploring Sandra's body in the big bed in the spare room until morning, when she fell asleep, sated, between her two lovers.

The hot sun was shining on her belly when she woke up, to find herself in a room cut out of the solid rock. She felt a hard penis pressed against her buttocks, and all the images of the past night flashed through her mind. She arched her back and nestled against Marc.

'I was watching you asleep. You're beautiful.'

'Mmm . . . hullo, Marc. Where's James? Making breakfast?'

'He's gone.'

Suddenly there was an inscrutable expression on Marc's face.

'How do you mean, *gone?* Gone where?'

'There was a phone call. He had to set off for Paris in a hurry – he asked me to tell you.'

Sandra said nothing. When Marc embraced her she opened her lips to him, responding to his caresses.

And a single tear trickled down her cheek.

II
MARC

4

Three in the morning. Montrose Place was deserted. Just as he did every evening, Police Constable Metcalf went into second gear before going up the slope and driving round the square slowly. He was paid to keep watch over the prosperous inhabitants of Belgravia, not to wake them up. The piercing yowl of a cat in search of a mate made him jump. He nudged his companion, Constable Bricknell, sitting beside him in the police car. They drew outside Number 6, a handsome Victorian house with a newly painted façade, and Metcalf looked up at the lighted windows of a room on the first floor.

'Bet they're having some fun up there!' he said with a guffaw, digging his elbow into the other man's ribs.

And just as he did every evening, Bricknell put up a silent prayer that when he got back to the station he would find the application for a transfer to the daytime shift, which he'd put in months ago, would have come through at last.

The dressing table lamp, a plain steel hemisphere, cast an unreal light on Marc Ronan's face. Eyes half-closed, jaws set, he was watching the smooth, shining, amber-coloured penis approaching Sandra. She was sitting naked on the white silk bedspread, with a pillow behind her back. Her wrists and ankles were tied to the bedposts with thin cords which Marc had knotted himself. Her breathing was hoarse and irregular. Marc felt the blood beating in his throat and temples. He swallowed his saliva and brushed Sandra's breast with one hand. She did not move, transfixed by the sight of the penis coming closer. Marc became bolder, and his fingers caressed the satiny texture of his wife's belly. She trembled, as if waking from a trance, and tried once again to struggle free of her bonds.

'Let me go, Marc!' she begged. 'Please! I don't want to . . .'

Her voice was so low it was almost a whisper.

'I don't want to!' she repeated without conviction.

'Oh yes, you do, Sandra! I know you want it. Look – you're all wet.'

As Marc spoke his hand plunged down between Sandra's thighs. Her cheeks went crimson with mingled excitement and shame. No, she *didn't* want Clapton to touch her. How could she give him her body tonight, and then pursue the mysteries of mathematics with him in the studious calm of the library tomorrow? But yes . . . she *did* want that penis steadily coming towards her, that vibrating length of flesh which seemed to get bigger and bigger as it approached its target. She shut her eyes so as not to see the man it belonged to, the man who had been teaching her maths and physics over the last month. Suddenly she thought that Marc must have chosen a black tutor for her solely with this evening in view. Then her thoughts blurred, she stopped struggling, and everything around her was mere sensation. She felt Marc's hands on her. She gave herself up to the familiar touch of them – their slightly rough but efficacious skill. Those fingers knew every corner of her body, knew where to linger, where to press harder or more lightly. Something brushed against her pubic hair. The black penis was just touching her. She moaned faintly. Her swollen emptiness ached, crying out for that male member.

Marc leaned over her and took her nipple in his mouth. The little button of flesh hardened. Sandra arched her body towards the other man's penis, from which a drop of liquid hung. But her bonds prevented her from moving. She would have to await the pleasure of that penis, Marc's pleasure, Clayton's pleasure. Now her hips were undulating uncontrollably. Her tongue licked over her lips. 'Oh yes, Marc, I want it!' she breathed, eyes still closed. 'Now! I want it, Marc!'

'Yes, my sweet,' he replied. 'Just be patient.'

Greedily, he sucked Sandra's breasts and stroked her clitoris. She felt a beating in her head, like a frantic heart-beat. Her legs, bound and stretched, hurt her. When Clapton's penis touched her moist flesh again she thought she was going to faint.

'Do it, Marc, please! Do it!'

She opened her eyes to see Marc delicately spreading her vaginal lips with one hand. With the other, he grasped the black man's gleaming penis and guided it into her. A cry of release escaped her. She felt herself surrounding the man, imprisoning him in her – for ever, it seemed. The penis now thrusting passionately inside her was the only thing attaching her to the phantom lover Marc wished to be the instrument of her pleasure. A black penis, and Marc's white hands on her body. She sought her husband's mouth while her hips followed the other man's movements, her ardent flesh responding to his as he thrust and plunged inside her. She was carried away by a cascade of orgasms, bursting out like tears kept back too long. Sandra cried out, and wept against Marc's cheek. He smiled. He had undone his trousers, and his fingers had brought out his penis. He was on the point of coming. He could not hold back any longer.

Deep within her, Sandra felt the pulsing that told her the other man was about to climax. Marc pressed his penis to her mouth, and she welcomed it in, rolling her tongue around the sensitive head, which was gorged with juice like a ripe fruit. As Clayton came inside her, Sandra swallowed Marc's sperm down to the very last drop.

Six in the morning. Metcalf had dropped Bricknell outside Charlie's cafe and left him there with a mug of hot coffee. Back in Montrose Place, still deserted, he went into second gear again. The car was slowly approaching Number 6, where the light was still on. Metcalf's little smile made his eyes disappear in the folds of his fat cheeks. When a door slammed he jumped. A young man was coming down the steps of Number 6, buttoning his shirt and carrying his jacket and tie. He looked dazed. When he saw the police car he shook himself, and strode off towards Halkin Street. Metcalf whistled quietly through his teeth.

'A black too!' he said, wishing Bricknell was there. 'She must be quite something, that little piece!'

Wearing a long, coral satin wrapper, and stifling a yawn, Sandra opened Marc's study door. She wondered how on earth her husband had been able to get up and go to work at the Embassy after his exciting night. She hadn't got up until two hours ago and was not quite sure that she was really awake yet.

'Marc, darling, Adèle says tea's ready.'

Renan put the receiver he had just lifted back on the phone. He rose, came round the desk and put his arms round Sandra.

'Hullo, my lovely.'

He kissed her tenderly, then turned her half-way round and gave her a little pat on the bottom. 'Go along, then, and I'll be with you.'

She blew him a soft kiss and glided out of the room.

The mere mention of Adèle was enough to irritate Marc. He should never have allowed Sandra to keep her on. He'd accepted the governess's presence at the start of their marriage, as a concession to his wife's youth, but he had never understood why Sandra wanted her. Was it to punish Adrien de Moncet, who was left alone in the big house at Rambouillet? Or was a way of bringing part of her own country with her? Yet he'd never thought Sandra was fond of old Adèle. And he did not like having her there to witness his married life. He would have preferred to have Sandra all to himself. When he made love to her, he felt as if the old woman were listening at the door. He must talk to Sandra about it again. So far, she had refused him nothing. Obedient Sandra. He remembered her sprawled body the night before, and a shiver ran through him. It was so easy to love her. Too easy, perhaps! He was sometimes surprised by the docility with which she let him arrange her life – the enthusiasm she showed in all circumstances (though still sometimes tinged with modesty), as if the fifteen years' difference in age between them meant he could never be wrong. Too easy? No, he thought not. He had been going carefully in their relationship, these last six months. He knew what passion and fire smouldered beneath that smooth exterior of Sandra's.

Marc shrugged his shoulders. Well, who knew – Adèle might serve his purpose in the long run! He dialled a number again, and spoke to someone at the other end of the line for three-quarters of a minute, before going to join his wife for tea.

Seven o'clock. Marc decided to go and see if Sandra was ready yet. She always took such a time to get dressed, he thought, smiling. But he dared not risk arriving late this evening of July 14th. The reception at the French Embassy was for eight-thirty, and whatever his private influence, a Second Secretary at the Embassy could not arrive after Lord Belcham, the British Foreign Minister. And Lord Belcham was never late.

Marc could not repress a shiver as he entered the big, black and white bedroom. He had given Sandra a free hand with the decoration, and sometimes regretted it. Severe lines, a chilly design – he found this stylized modernity almost vulgar at times, and yet it aroused him. His own contribution had been to add long panels of mirrors on the wall facing the bed and over half the ceiling. Given the mirrors, the room fulfilled its functions very well.

Sandra saw him. She was standing in front of one of the mirrors, and she spun round and smiled at him.

'You look magnificent!' he said dropping a kiss on the base of her throat.

He let his eyes travel over the black dress with its narrow shoulder straps. It clung to Sandra like a second skin. He noticed that she was wearing heavy gold bracelets on both wrists to hide the marks left by their games last night.

'Maybe,' said Sandra, sulkily, 'but I'm not ready yet.'

He drew her to him, his hands passing over her firm

body. He found her mouth and kissed her hard.

'If you go on like that we're *sure* to be late!'

Marc had slipped his hand under the long slit in the side of her dress. It was travelling up her thigh. Then, suddenly, it stopped.

'How do you expect me to think of this reception when you're not wearing knickers?' he whispered into Sandra's ear.

He lifted the dress, exposing his wife's long legs. She was wearing nothing under it but sheer black stockings and a lacy suspender belt which made an exquisite frame for her fleece of auburn hair. Marc's eyes clung to that triangle of hair as if they wanted to penetrate it.

'The loveliest thing in the world,' he murmured dreamily. 'And all at my disposal – I only have to reach out my hand. I like to know you're available, Sandra.'

'And I always will be – for you.'

'For other men too. For everyone.'

He seemed to see, once again, the black penis plunging into Sandra's pearly white body.

'Marc,' she said gently, 'I really *must* finish getting ready.'

With a graceful movement, she freed herself and turning, showing her rounded white buttocks. Still holding her dress up to her hips, she walked over to the dressing table before letting the silky material fall again. She sat down.

Marc gave himself a little shake.

'Yes, you're right,' he said, going to the door.

Sandra looked at him in surprise. It usually took more than that to make Marc give up an idea – particularly an idea of *that* sort! Perhaps he was more worried about the reception than he seemed? She blew him a kiss.

'I'll see you soon, Sandra.' A strange light was kindled in his green eyes. 'Don't keep me waiting.'

Sandra readjusted the straps of her dress. The satin sliding over her bare shoulders was a delicious sensation. She loved to wear her dresses with nothing underneath, next to her skin. 'That's another thing Marc has taught me,' she thought, picking up a powder puff. A haze of fine powder drifted from it.

The rectangular mirror showed her reflection. Hand poised in the air, she tried to read her face, looking for some mark of what had happened last night – what had happened on so many past nights.

Just a year, she told her reflection: have I really changed?

Her skin was as fresh as ever, her mouth as soft. Her body had blossomed under masculine caresses. Nothing but an occasional look in her violet eyes showed a crack in that beautifully varnished surface. It was twelve months since she woke that morning in Juan-les-Pins, abruptly returned to a reality she couldn't and still didn't understand. Neither Marc nor Adrien could throw any light on the mystery! James Llewelyn had simply disappeared, and no one knew where he was. Adrien seemed annoyed, Marc seemed worried, but she kept on meeting a wall of silence. Was Marc, the last person to see James, really telling the truth? She hadn't wanted to believe him at first. She had shut herself in her room and cried for days on end. Rambouillet and all its conventions closed round her again. Marc respected this symbolic mourning period. Adrien said nothing. No doubt they both knew what she felt for James, but they chose to ignore her feelings.

Then, one day, Marc came back. And she clung to him, despite her father's disapproval, as if to an image of lost happiness. He brought something in her she had thought dead back to life. And one clear December day she chose the way she thought led to freedom. Marc loved her.

'Getting married? At sixteen? My dear, you're crazy!' Lucy had cried, eyes popping out of her head.

It wasn't long before the news was all round their school. Everyone looked at her as if she had the plague!

Adrien had not given in willingly.

'It's unnatural,' he said. 'You're too young, and Renan is fifteen years older. Your mother –''

'Well, *she* was sixteen when she married you, wasn't she?'

'That has nothing to do with it!'

Sandra was asking herself a number of questions. It was almost as if her father, after practically throwing her into the arms of the two young men, realized that the game had gone too far. As if he, himself, didn't understand just when the whole thing had gone beyond his control. But Sandra had made her decision, and in the end Adrien gave way.

After that everything happened very fast. There was the wedding ceremony; she'd had an urge to laugh right through it. All the respectable members of the family looking at her so disapprovingly, cackling that there was no smoke without fire. Gregory was stranded somewhere the other side of the world and couldn't come. Sandra was almost relieved. He merely sent her a Jaguar with an enormous white ribbon round it, and a little card saying *You know how to drive now, Tsarina.*

Marc had just been appointed to the French Embassy in London, and they moved to the British capital directly after their wedding. Her father had written just once in six months, and she had not replied.

'Well, now I come to think of it, I *have* changed!' she told herself, putting down the powder puff. Thanks to Marc, thanks to this exciting city! She had started to become what she wanted to be – a woman free to dispose of herself as she liked.

Sandra looked at the little clock on the dressing table. Nearly eight. She searched frantically for the browny-red lipstick which set off her complexion so well. But her mind was elsewhere. She was re-living her first impressions of London, her strolls down Carnaby Street, the passion she had developed for rock music, the roar and bustle of the city – such an eye-opener after the placidity of life at Rambouillet. The more she opened her mind to the vibes of London the more her sensual appetite grew. And Marc had taken great pains to encourage it, without ever entirely satisfying it. He had turned out to be an extraordinary lover: imaginative, curious, protective. He wanted to teach her everything. Bit by bit, Sandra's modesty and sense of shame melted away. It began with the tutors Marc engaged for her. None of them stayed very long. Variety may not be the best way of teaching maths or philosophy – but it is the only way to learn the art of love.

Then, while she was walking in Holland Park one day, a fair young man with shoulder-length hair accosted her. He took her down an alley and into a big, dusty room full of newspapers where three other young men were drinking beer and laughing. They were passing round a tapering cigarette, larger than an ordinary one, and when the blond man offered it to her Sandra hesitated only for a second. She was discovering hash and the underworld both at once. Later, when the blond man made love to her on piles of unsold newspapers among the lumber at the back of the room, she discovered new sensations in the cloud of greenish smoke that seemed to surround them – sensations more acute and lasting longer than any she had known before.

When she got back to Montrose Place she told Marc all about it, perhaps expecting a violent reaction, some sign of jealousy. Instead, Marc took her in his arms, asked her to tell him about her adventure all over again, not leaving any details out, and then he had her on the drawing room carpet without undressing,her, seeking the stranger's odour and the way he had gone on her body.

Sandra shivered at the memory.

'I'm not giving you a moment longer!'

Marc had just come in. She smiled at him, picked up her black evening bag, and they left the bedroom holding hands.

Montrose Place was only a few hundred yards from Knightsbridge, but when they came out on to the steps Sandra saw that the Daimler provided by the Embassy for Marc's use was waiting.

'Why don't we walk for a change, Marc?' she suggested. 'It's such a fine evening!'

'Certainly not. Do you see us arriving like a couple of nobodies, perspiring and carrying a change of shoes? Come on, get in.'

'Marc, you're exaggerating!' But she slipped into the passenger seat.

Slowly, Marc turned into Halkin Street and then into Grosvenor Crescent. 'I'm not exaggerating at all,' he remarked, making Sandra jump. She had been lost in thought. 'The cream of the Foreign Office will be there this evening, and I want you to do me credit.'

'Oh . . . and just how does my lord and master wish me to do that?' murmured Sandra, placing her long fingers on Marc's thigh.

He laughed. 'Little pest! You really do begin to please me – you're a quick learner!'

She crossed her hands over her breasts and made him a little bow in imitation of a geisha girl.

'Anything for the greater pleasure of my lord and master!' she replied.

Then she noticed that instead of turning into Knightsbridge, the Daimler had gone off towards Hyde Park Corner and was now driving down Park Lane.

'Marc, my poor darling! You've lost your memory.' She passed a hand over his forehead. 'That must be it, you're feverish! You've forgotten the way to your own Embassy!'

Her eyes were sparkling with mischief as she laid her hand on Marc's leg again and moved it up towards his crotch, where an interesting bulge was appearing.

Marc said nothing, but tried to keep a straight face. The lighted signs above the big hotels were speeding past, casting red and white reflections on the Daimler's smoked glass windows. They entered Hyde Park through the Victoria Gate. Marc slowed down. Now Sandra knew why her husband had not been more pressing, back in their bedroom!

'Very well – my hour of vengeance has come!' he told her solemnly.

And with great dignity, still holding the steering wheel with one hand, he quickly opened his trousers. Without more ado, he pulled Sandra's head down to his penis. A willing victim, she did as he wanted and took the erect penis between her lips, with a little sigh. Marc shuddered and put his foot on the brake. Sandra's tongue was diabolically skilful. She caressed the head of his penis, sucked it in, licked all round it, drawing hoarse little moans from him. The Daimler was crawling along very slowly now. Marc looked down at the cascade of auburn hair flowing over his lower abdomen, and the sight brought fire to his loins.

He let go of the wheel and closed his eyes. Both his hands were resting on Sandra's head. He felt the heat of the sperm rising in his penis.

'Watch out!'

Instinctively, he stood on the brake. The Daimler gave a jolt and then stood still. Marc opened his eyes. A middle-aged couple were staring at him with their eyes popping out of their heads, like a pair of rabbits caught in the beam of his headlights.

Marc lowered the window and cleared his throat. Sandra's mouth was still fastened to him.

"Road hog!' said the man. 'You might look where you're going!'

He marched up to the car, followed by his companion.

'You might have killed us!' the woman yelped, leaning through the open window towards Marc like an avenging Fury. 'But this won't be the last you hear of it! We shall complain to the police, we shall . . .'

Suddenly she seemed to choke.

Sandra had just looked up at her, clear-eyed, with Marc's penis still in her mouth – it grew even larger.

'A sex maniac! Help!' cried the woman, turning to run and dragging her startled companion with her.

'Police! Help! Police!'

Her shouts died away. Marc and Sandra looked at each other and burst out laughing.

'We'd better move away from here! Can't you just see the headlines tomorrow morning? Hyde Park Sex Fiends: French diplomat and young female accomplice found frightening single women and respectable couples!'

He drew the Daimler up under an elm at the roadside.

Half an hour later, a black car drew up outside Number 58, Knightsbridge. Elegant, relaxed and self-assured, the Second Secretary and his young wife got out, a glow of pleasure still shining in their eyes.

Martin, the major-domo, stood very stiff and straight at the top of the flight of stairs leading to the big reception room. Marc and Sandra Renan passed him, hurrying in. All the other members of the Embassy staff were already there, waiting restlessly for the guests. It was twenty-seven minutes past eight.

Marc quietly greeted his colleagues, and paid his respects to M. de Vignes, the Ambassador, under the choleric eye of the military attaché. General Brignon, a very correct character, deplored the casual manners of young French diplomats these days.

Sandra had joined a group of other Embassy wives. They were exchanging the latest gossip and complimenting each other on their dresses, with acid smiles. Sandra didn't care for the diplomats' ladies: they were a curious caste, steeped in hypocrisy, and they struck her as being unable to appreciate the real pleasures of life.

'My dear, your dress is simply divine!' bleated the legal adviser's wife. 'Though a little – well – revealing! What do *you* think, Mme Berthier? Of course, when one is as young as Mme Renan . . . '

'I think Sandra looks lovely! She's about the only person here who could wear that sort of dress without looking like what you have in mind, dear Mme Robin!'

The speaker was the Ambassador's personal secretary, a tall, pretty blonde called Nancy Gaylord, the only woman here Sandra really liked. She was straightforward and intelligent. The two girls, one English and one French, had taken to each other immediately.

Mme Robin nearly swallowed her pearl necklace. Luckily, Martin was announcing the first guests, a small group of Foreign Office functionaries, putting an end to this feminine confrontation for the time being. Cards were piling up in the major-domo's hand. Gradually, the big room filled. The Maître d'hotel gave discreet orders to white-clad waiters standing ready at the buffet tables.

'His Excellency Lord Belcham!' announced Martin in a carrying voice.

'Our undercover agent's in good voice this evening,' Marc murmured to Jounot, the young cultural attaché.

All the Embassy staff knew that Martin carried a revolver under his livery. The security services will use any form of cover for their men, and the least obvious are often the best.

Along with his wife, the British Foreign Minister made his entrance, monocle in hand, moustache bristling. M. de Vignes hurried to welcome him, and after the usual polite exchanges the evening became a little less formal. Champagne was loosening the guests' tongues, and strict etiquette wore thin at the edges.

Sandra and Nancy Gaylord were talking to Jounot, who was trying to explain the London underworld to them. Sandra couldn't help smiling at his enthusiasm. Jounot was a budding writer who had managed to get himself this posting for the period of his military service, and he sometimes tended to take himself rather seriously.

'So far as magazines are concerned, *Oz* is the one! Their method, you understand, is to . . . '

'Oh, my dear Pierre, you talk too much!' said Nancy. 'Try thinking of something else!' And she drew him towards the terrace. 'Talking about magazines, have you heard of *Suck?*'

Sandra watched the tall blonde, whose eyes were resting indulgently on the moon-faced little writer.

Well, she said to herself, repressing a mischievous smile, I wonder how those two will finish the evening! She looked round the room. Marc seemed to be deep in conversation with Lady Belcham, and she decided not to disturb them. She looked down at her empty glass and made for the nearest buffet table.

A hand was laid on her arm.

'Good evening, Mlle de Moncet – or not, it's Mme Renan now, isn't it?'

Sandra turned round, and saw a gold sheath dress clinging to a voluptuously contoured figure. Two black eyes were looking into hers, and a sweet perfume hung in the air.

'May!' Sandra could have hugged her, but remembered where she was just in time. 'May, what are you doing here? Why didn't you let me know? Where's Gregory?'

She looked eagerly round.

'One question at a time, Sandra!' said May, laughing. 'Gregory's in Singapore, and I'm here seeing one of his clients.'

'I didn't know you worked with him.'

'Let's say he's the iron hand – and I'm his velvet glove.'

'I see.'

'I'm not so sure you do . . . but in any case, I only arrived this afternoon, and since we were coming to this reception and I knew you'd be here, I thought I'd surprise you.'

'We?'

'I'm with General Saunders. The man over there weighed down by his medals and boring Lord Belcham.'

She pointed a red-lacquered nail discreetly at the far end of the room. Sandra saw a tallish man with a prominent paunch. He had a long, thin nose, and his eyebrows met in a severe line. She remembered seeing him that evening on the *Rosebud*.

'May, let's leave!' she said suddenly. 'I'm sick of these society gatherings.'

May shot her a surprised look, but did not argue.

'Very well. I'll go and tell the General, and we'll meet on the steps outside.'

Sandra found Marc and detached him from a group of

admirers: four stout and talkative Englishwomen.

'Marc, I've got the most dreadful headache! I'm going home. Would you apologize to everyone for me?'

'Sandra, what is it? Wait a moment – if you're not feeling well I'll take you home.'

'No, don't bother. May's going with me. You remember her, don't you? A friend of Gregory's – we met on the *Rosebud*.'

Marc did not seem very pleased, but Sandra turned to the big door, where a black and gold figure was signalling to her.

'Yes, I remember her,' said Marc. 'I'll see you later, then.'

Pensively, he watched the two women walk away.

'I can't make you out, Sandra. A little while ago you were sparkling – and now you look as if you had the cares of the world on your shoulders."

Sitting comfortably back on the silk-covered sofa in the drawing room, May was delicately sipping gin. Sandra watched the movement of her pointed pink tongue as it dipped into the transparent liquid. She felt cross with herself for giving way to the melancholy mood that had suddenly come over her. May, General Saunders, the *Rosebud* – the memories were rather too much for one evening.

'Come over here and sit beside me.' May straightended up to make room for the younger woman, who rose from her chair and sat down on the sofa. May put her arm round Sandra's shoulders. 'Well, what's wrong? I might be able to help you. Aren't you happy with Marc?'

Sandra's only reply was to burst into tears. They streamed down her cheeks. Shaken by sobs, she hid her face against May's welcoming shoulder.

'There now, Tsarina – have a good cry!'

May stroked her hair and murmured comforting words into her ear. Sandra stayed like that for ten minutes, ridding her body of all the pain of the past. May kissed her cheek, and she nestled closer to her gentle friend, breathing in May's jasmine perfume. She felt good. Nothing mattered any more except that hand on the back of her neck, on her shoulder. The strap of her dress slipped off, and May put her lips to the smooth hollow at the base of Sandra's throat. Sandra trembled. Her body did not ache any more. Not for anything in the world would she have drawn away from the warmth of that skin next to hers.

May's mouth traced the line of her throat, reached the cleft between her breasts. Head thrown back, Sandra moaned.

'May . . . ' she began, trying to look into the other woman's eyes. And then, huskily: 'I think I want to . . . '

May put a finger on her lips. 'Hush, Sandra. Some things don't need to be explained – you must just enjoy them.'

Her mouth moved to Sandra's trembling lips, and Sandra gave herself up to the skilful sweetness of May's tongue. It was the first time she had ever kissed a woman, and at that moment she felt so totally happy she wished she hadn't waited so long.

'Let's go up to my room.'

Shyly, she took May's hand and led her to the mirror-lined sanctum.

But once the door was closed behind them, Sandra did not seem to know what to do next. May came up to her, embraced her tenderly again, and led her to the bed, stroking her breasts.

'Wait – don't lie down yet. I want to look at you.' And just like Marc earlier in the evening, May lifted Sandra's dress. She knelt in front of the girl's nakedness. 'I want to taste you . . . eat you!'

May stroked Sandra's long, firm thighs. Her mouth moved over the girl's skin. Sandra was holding her dress up to her waist, revelling in the sight. May was exploring her fleece of hair, delicately nibbling the folds of her groin. Hands on Sandra's buttocks, she rubbed her face against the silky auburn hair. Her tongue went further, wriggling into the damp cleft of the vulva, finding the most sensitive places, licking it, leaving it, coming back to it again.

'May, I *must* lie down!' Sandra gasped.

She let herself fall back on the bed. May's mouth still clung to her lower lips, and the sensations it was giving her were something so new and different that she came almost at once. Her body arched up, seemed to hover in the air for a moment, and then dropped back on the bed. May lay down beside her, while Sandra savoured the pleasure she had just discovered, getting used to the idea of it.

'Now *you* get undressed,' she said to May a few minutes later. She was taking off her own dress and her suspender belt and stockings. 'I want to stroke you, too.'

Without hesitation, May slipped out of her golden sheath, revealing tanned skin, rounded hips and full breasts.

'You're beautiful!' said Sandra, taking one of the brown nipples in her mouth. She found she knew instinctively what movements and caresses would bring her friend to orgasm – she only had to remember the details of her own pleasure just now.

She raised May's hips like an arch, with her fingers underneath them. The blood was beating in her temples. She felt as if a dam had given way within her.

Shaking back her hair, she put her face to the slit lying exposed to her, intoxicating herself with the fragrance of their mingled juices.

Mouth open, she plunged between May's thighs, licking the mount of Venus with little strokes of her tongue. May writhed on the bed, her head tossing from left to right. 'Sandra, my little virgin – lick me, yes, harder! Oh, I shall come!'

Sandra's mouth devoured the dripping vulva, found and fastened on the little button of the clitoris, which swelled and throbbed under her own saliva. May's body was shaken by spasms; she pulled the girl's auburn mane even closer. 'Sandra, you'll drive me crazy!'

Sandra was carried away, as if she were making love to her own reflection. She nibbled, licked and sucked, and May moved rhythmically in time to her own movements.

'I'm coming – oh, that's so good!' May cried.

And at once she lay close to Sandra and began stroking her again. Sandra's aching genitals welcomed the touch of her hand. Nothing but the panting of the two women broke the silence of the room, while the mirrors reflected their entwined bodies to infinity.

'Look at yourself, Sandra!' said May. 'I want you to watch me taking you.'

Glancing at the ceiling mirror, Sandra saw May push two fingers up her dripping vagina.

She let out a hoarse cry. 'Yes, take me – harder!'

May's fingers were working vigorously away inside her.

'Do it again – again – faster!' cried Sandra, as the improvised penis thrust into her. Her hips rose towards the ceiling.

'May, kiss me . . . oh, May!'

She saw herself come to climax in the mirror.

Clinging together, they waited for the hurricane they had unleashed to die down.

'Congratulations, Tsarina. For a beginner, you're very gifted! Or perhaps this isn't your first time with a woman?'

'Yes, it is – and I'm so glad the first time is with *you*, May!'

'Oh, already imagining the long list of my successors, are you? Well, if you're as good with men as with women, I can see you have a fine career in the erotic arts ahead of you!'

'Would you like to be my manager?' asked Sandra, laughing.

'Why not?' said May. 'I might well come to think your uncle had second sight when he nicknamed you Tsarina, and even Catherine the Great herself couldn't compete!'

'And I'm only seventeen – what will you say in a few years' time?'

Teasingly, Sandra brushed her hand over her friend's

lower lips, and then, becoming serious again, said, 'May, I want to ask you a great favour.'

'After this evening, how can I refuse you anything?'

'No, listen, this is very serious. I want you to find James Llewelyn.'

'What?' Abruptly, May sat up. 'So, that's it – that's what's bothering you!'

'Don't get the wrong idea, May. I'm perfectly happy. It's just curiosity – I want to know *why* he disappeared.'

'Just curiosity?' repeated May, doubtfully.

'Well, think whatever you like. Call it injured pride, anything – but help me find him.'

At that moment, soundlessly, the door opened. The carpet muffled the newcomer's footsteps.

'What a pretty sight! Any room for me in this charming group?' asked Marc.

The two women gave a start. May was the first to recover herself.

'As far as *I'm* concerned, I think I've had my quota of orgasms for tonight,' she said, getting to her feet. Bending down to pick up her dress, she did not see the sinister shadow which momentarily veiled Marc's eyes.

Sandra wondered just how long he had been standing there on the other side of the door.

5

The elegant little notebook in its red leather cover, a present from Gregory, suddenly struck Sandra as futile. She couldn't help thinking how neatly its pages summed up her life since she had left London. M.C., Zürich; K.J., Bonn; A.C., Rome; J.B.F., Helsinki. The initials danced a melancholy round before her eyes. Oh yes, she had had them all! The military attaché in Italy, the legal adviser in — Scandinavia, that First Secretary, the one with such melting eyes, in Poland, the commercial delegate – well, she couldn't quite remember where! So many countries over such a short period! For the first time, she was asking herself some questions. *Why* all these moves? Marc's vague explanations didn't satify her. He forgot she was an ambassador's daughter, and knew quite well that the term "special attaché" could cover anything and everything.

What exactly was he doing, going from Embassy to Embassy? She sometimes got the impression that his only purpose in all these travels was to extend the list of her lovers, showing her off to all the members of the French Diplomatic Service in the four corners of Europe. It was as if Marc had decided that those tutors he had engaged for her education were not enough any more: something more substantial was needed. But no – she'd never told him about her affair with L.W. in Warsaw. That was a memory she treasured for itself: a little haven of peace in a whirlpool of events which was becoming bewildering to her.

She rose from the depths of the leather armchair and went towards the library, running a nervous hand through her hair. Why did she feel as if she were stifling in this appartment? Was it because she'd travelled so much, these last two years, she couldn't live any more without a suitcase ready to hand?

She heard the sound of a chair being pushed back in the next room. Marc had been shut away in his study for three hours. She'd hardly seen him this morning – and now she came to think of it, it struck her that since their return to Paris and the Renan family apartment in the Avenue des Ternes, they had hardly done more than meet in passing like a couple of strangers.

Marc opened the drawing room door.

'Sandra darling, I'm lunching with Dambier. I'll be spending the afternoon at the Foreign Office, so don't wait around for me.'

'All right.'

'Can't you go and see a girl friend or something?'

'Yes, sure, Marc. Don't worry about me.'

He kissed her forehead in an absent-minded way, took his overcoat off the hook in the hall and went out, briefcase in hand.

She didn't have any girl friends. Her friends from her schooldays might have existed in another century. She had met May again by chance in London, but now she had rejoined Gregory on his yacht, roaming the world. Even the faithful Adèle had deserted her once they left London: Marc had convinced her that she couldn't stand the pace of all their diplomatic travels, so the governess went back to Adrien at Rambouillet, to nurse his arithritis and preside over the sacred ceremony of the tea-table.

Sandra felt lonelier than she had ever been in her life – even in her worst moments at Rambouillet. Marc himself seemed to be avoiding her. Was the man who had loved her – or so she thought – tired of her already? She'd married him to escape her gilded cage and her memories, and here she was once again, back in a kind of prison, brooding on a past she would rather have forgotten.

What was she going to do today? And the day after, and the day after that? What was she going to do with her life?

If only May were here – or Nancy Gaylord, the young Englishwoman she had liked so much! But she was alone in the apartment with little Marie, the maid, who seemed so devoted to Marc. A vision rose in her mind's eye and was quickly banished: Marc and Marie on the kitchen table . . . yes, surely they'd done it before Marc married her. Perhaps they still did.

Suddenly she knew why she disliked this apartment so much. It bore the marks of another woman's hand, in all sorts of paltry little details. In their bedroom, Marc's things were neatly tidied away and there was always a rose on his bedside table. But most of the time Sandra had to deal with her own clothes, and *she* got no flowers. It was the same in the bathroom, the study, even the drawing room, where Marc's favourite armchair always seemed to be carefully brushed! Briefly, Sandra noticed whether these little signs really existed, or if her troubled mind had conjured them up. It was crazy! A daughter of the de Moncet family, supplanted by a little maidservant?

She didn't want to think about it any more. She fetched her coat from the dressing room and went out, slamming the door.

Oddly enough, she found the noise in the street soothing. All around her, the bustling city was alive. She walked towards the Place des Ternes and tuned into the Rue du Faubourg St Honoré. She walked on for a long time, without any precise idea of where she was going, before noticing that a man was following her. And perhaps *had* been following her for some time. Slightly uneasy, she quickened her pace. The man went on following. He wore an elegant overcoat and a soft hat. He looked like a businessman of about forty, and in other circumstances she might have been interested in him. Just now, however, without knowing why, she started to run. The man stepped out more briskly. The Rue de La Baume was deserted.

Without thinking, Sandra pushed open the outer door of an apartment building and found herself under a dark archway. Breathless, she leaned back against the wall and tried to calm the beating of her heart.

It's all right, she told herself, he's gone past now. Only someone trying to pick up a girl. Calm down, Sandra!

She heard the thud of the outer door again. It was opening. In the thin ray of light, she recognized the stranger.

'Leave me alone!' she cried. 'Go away!'

The door had closed again, and there was darkness all round her.

'Hush, hush, mademoiselle!' murmured the man. 'I won't harm you.'

'Why were you following me just now?'

His laughter echoed in the archway. 'As it happens, mademoiselle, I live here. No doubt you live here too?'

Sandra heaved a deep sigh of relief. Something seemed to snap inside her. He lived here! You fool, she told herself, what an idiot you are! She felt quite faint – her head was swimming. The man was close to her now.

'Can't you find the light switch for the stairs?' he asked.

A strange sense of languor came over Sandra. She felt unable to react, as if fear and the sudden realization that she had been alarmed for nothing had paralysed her muscles and her mind. The man was even closer now. She could smell him, and the citrus fragrance of his aftershave.

She could hardly breathe. Put on the light, she thought – I must put on the light, at once!

A hand touched her. She couldn't move. The man was pulling her to him, holding her against his chest. She tried to resist, but found that her body was tightly clutched to the strangers. A mouth searched for hers, and found it. She responded to the embrace with a frenzy that startled her. A moan escaped her. Her stomach was churning; her pelvis was held close to the man's penis, and she could tell he had an erection.

Rapidly, he undid his overcoat, opened the front of Sandra's dress and roughly massaged one breast. She clung to her invisible partner's loins. The stranger put a hand on her thigh, removed her panties, and penetrated her without any other preliminaries. His penis plunged into her, hurting her. She bent her knees, clasped the man's hips between her thighs, and felt the penis go farther in. Then, with one last effort, she tried to pull away – but the stranger had her impaled there, and was thrusting away inside her with a vigour and violence she had never known before.

Tears rolled down Sandra's cheeks.

'Stop it!' she cried – and then, between her sobs, 'You're hurting me – oh – oh, that's good!'

Despite herself, her body was shaken by spasms. As the man discharged long, burning streams of sperm, she came to climax without a sound. Her legs would not support her any more, and the stranger had to hold her up while he finished coming himself.

Sandra abruptly regained her self-control and shook herself, as if waking from a bad dream. The man loosened his grip.

'Very good! You're wonderful!'

She tore herself out of his arms and rushed to the door. The bright light out in the street blinded her for a moment, and then she began to run. Her face was streaming with tears, and at every step she took she felt the man's sperm running down her thighs.

By the time she opened the door of the apartment in the Avenue des Ternes, Sandra had stopped crying. She went straight to the bathroom, locked herself in, and stayed there for an hour, trying to wash the sense of defilement off her body. There was nothing in her mind now but immense disgust – for herself, for men in general, for life itself.

Swathed in a long wrapper, she dropped into one of the armchairs in the drawing room, a glass of gin in her hand. The alcohol had a numbing effect. When Marie came in with a salver, Sandra had almost regained her composure.

'A telegram came for you, madame,' said the maid, holding out the salver.

With a languid hand, Sandra took the blue rectangle.

'Thank you, Marie. You may go.'

She waited for the door to close again before opening the telegram. Who could have sent it? Adrien? Did he even know she was in Paris? Gregory? The idea was enough to galvanize her into action. She sat up, put her glass down on a pedestal table, and unfolded the telegram. Her fingers were not trembling any more.

Have found J. Expect you in Casablanca on the 8th. Will meet Air France Flight 309 arriving 21 hours, and AF Flight 312 arriving 23 hours. Love, M.

She had to read the message several times before its meaning sank in. Then her mind worked very fast. Found J? Found James! May! May had found James and was expecting her in Casablanca! Sandra could hardly think straight. Tuesday, Wednesday, Thursday . . . the 8th. The 8th was today! In sudden panic, she got up and checked the date on the calendar in her diary.

That meant May was expecting her in Casablanca this evening. Could she possibly make it? How? Her head was going round and round. She didn't know which way to start tackling the problem. And why Casablanca? Why hadn't May come to Paris? Suddenly a doubt came into her mind. May *must* know she was tied to Marc – she couldn't just set out at a moment's notice when May snapped her fingers! So why the telegram? It didn't make sense. Unless – unless James himself was in Casablanca! Yes, that must be it: James *was* in Casablanca. That was the only possible explanation.

What was the time? Her brain was a blank, except for one single thought that filled it: the flight arriving at 23 hours.

She glanced at her watch. Yes, as she'd thought, it was already too late to catch the earlier flight. She lit a cigarette. For once, she was glad Marc was not home yet. She went over to the telephone, turned the pages of the directory, and dialled a number.

'Air France? Can I have a seat on Flight 312 to Casablanca? Yes – yes, I'll hang on. Thank you.'

The plane took off at 17.45 hours. She would just have time to fling some clothes into a suitcase and scribble a few words for Marc. She wouldn't exactly lie: she'd tell him May had sent her a telegram and was in Morocco, in some kind of trouble, and she'd be back herself in a few days' time. He would understand – or maybe he *wouldn't* understand, but she suddenly realized that she didn't mind.

In her room she changed into a lightweight outfit, but decided to take her fur coat. She slipped the telegram into her handbag.

Then she went into Marc's study, wrote a quick note, put it in an envelope and left it conspicuously propped against a lamp.

She left the study, closing the door carefully behind her. A quick glance told her that Marie was not about.

Then she was out on the landing, breathless. A dull ache of fear gripped her heart, and she had to lean against the wall for a moment. Suppose she met Marc now? He had been behaving so oddly since their return to Paris – she feared the worst. How could she excuse this escapade of hers, which looked as if she were running away?

But there was no one on the stairs. She hailed the first taxi to pass the door and sank gratefully into it.

'Orly,' she breathed.

The Boeing 727 was still climbing when the No Smoking sign went out, and Sandra began to breathe normally again. She couldn't help feeling slightly alarmed whenever she was in a plane taking off or landing. The air hostesses bustled about like busy little ants. Sandra closed her eyes and leaned her head against the back of her seat. Now she was actually on her way to Casablanca, she could try to sort her thoughts out.

The girl at the Air France desk had explained that she was in luck. The flight was fully booked, but one passenger had cancelled at the last minute.

Was it really luck? What was she doing in this plane, chasing a phantom? And suppose she had just ruined the relationship between herself and Marc – or what could still be salvaged of it – for good?

She tried imagining Marc's reaction to her note. He might be furious.

'Would you like anything to drink, mademoiselle?'

The air hostess was dark and pretty, and had a soft voice like May's.

'No, thank you.'

The old Englishwoman seated on Sandra's right had ordered a whisky, which she drank with a series of irritating little noises. Sandra closed her eyes again. James's face, blurred by the passage of time, rose behind her eyelids. Was she really about to see him again? Somehow or other she just couldn't believe it.

Exhausted, Sandra suddenly dropped off into a dreamless sleep.

'We have just landed at Casablanca. The time is 23 hours. The temperature outside is twenty-two degrees. Captain Mathieu and the crew hope you have enjoyed your flight.'

The syrupy voice brought Sandra back to reality. She realized that she must have slept right through the flight – however, now she felt rested, calm, and ready to face what awaited her. She tidied herself up a little, checked her mascara in the small mirror in her bag, and followed the crowd of passengers towards the ramp going down to the ground.

The air was surprisingly mild. A scent of jasmine seemed to float as far as the tarmac. Still following her travelling companions, Sandra found herself in a modern, brightly lit building. Arrows pointed the way to the baggage collection point. Behind a barrier, a motley crowd of people was waiting for the passengers. Veiled women, men wearing the Arab burnous, Arabs in Western dress, tourists got up as Moslems. She scanned them and realized, with disappointment, that May was not there.

She may be in the bar, she told herself hopefully. Her own case came round on the conveyor belt; she picked it up, refused the offers of a porter, and made her way to the cafeteria, where she sat down at a table and ordered coffee. She decided to wait for half an hour. When the waiter brought her coffee she gave him a detailed description of May.

'Have you seen anyone who looks like that? She was supposed to be meeting me at the airport this evening.'

'Sorry, mademoiselle, I can't say that I have. But you know, I see so many people . . . '

Sandra felt abandoned. She had never been alone in a foreign country before, and wasn't really sure she knew how to manage. How would she ever find May in a city she did not know?

She drank the hot coffee all at once, and went to find the messages board. There was nothing for her there. She asked the official at the little window next to it, 'Excuse me, is there a message for Mme Renan, by any chance?'

'Wait a minute. I'll check . . . no, I'm sorry, madame.'

'Mlle de Moncet, perhaps?'

'No, I'm sorry, nothing for that name either.'

'Thank you. I want to leave a message myself, please.'

The man gave her a form, and she hurriedly scribbled a message for May Campbell. *Will be at the Hilton – there must be a Hilton here. Sandra.*

She took a last look round, and then finally decided to leave the airport. She was walking to the taxi rank when a little man in a white suit and hat came up to her. Sandra saw that he had long, silvery hair brushed back from his face, a black tie, and dark eyes above a hooked nose. His mouth shook slightly as he spoke.

'Mme Renan?'

'Yes, that's me,' she replied, surprised.

'Mme Campbell sends her apologies. She couldn't come herself. She has asked me to drive you to where she is staying. If you'll follow me . . .'

'Oh, thank you.'

Suddenly Sandra was not frightened any more. May hadn't forgotten her! The world looked familiar again. She was so relieved that she did not notice the Diplomatic Corps plate on the sedan with the black upholstery which drew up beside her. Any more than she noticed another passenger already in the car when the little man in white opened the rear door for her.

By the time she saw the white piece of wadding, it was too late. A strong hand pulled her in and held the improvised mask down on her face. She struggled for a moment or so, and then darkness overcame her.

Somewhere, soft music was playing. In her head. With difficulty, she opened her swollen eyes, but she could not see anything. She felt as if her mouth were made of wood, and there was a most unpleasant taste in it. Chloroform. Her memory came back to her in disjointed scraps. The airport, the telegram, a car, the little man in white. She tried to sit up. Gradually, her eyes became more used to the dark. She was in a room furnished entirely in red, on a large bed with a black satin cover. Her eyes travelled round the room, seeing the walls hung with red velvet, the sofa piled high with small cushions, the dark wood table where a large bouquet of red roses was arranged in an opaline vase, the heavy curtains that half hid the windows. An armchair had a wrapper thrown over its back. The door was closed. A faint light came from a shaded bedside lamp on her left, and she suddenly saw a face leaning over her.

'Who are you?' she asked. 'What *is* this place? Why have I been brought here?'

She hardly believed it all as she spoke. A voice in her head kept saying: this is only a bad dream, a nightmare, that's all. Soon I'll wake up and everything will be back to normal.

The face came to life. A red mouth stood out against the pallor of the skin, and the black eyes were ice-cold. Cruel eyes.

'You don't ask any questions from now on, Sandra,' said a deep slightly husky voice. 'You're here to obey. To work.'

The woman rose to her feet. Sandra saw that she was tall and thin. Her black hair was pulled back in the nape of her neck, and two heavy gold rings hung from her ears. She was smoking a cigarette in a holder. The aroma of the scented tobacco filled the room. Her red dress, clinging to her figure, revealed a boylike torso but a woman's hips.

'You're crazy!' was all Sandra said.

She tried to get up, but a shooting pain made her lay her head back on the pillow.

'Ah, good! Very good! We like restive fillies here!'

'Where's May? Tell me – I insist on knowing! I want to telephone. Marc will come, he'll know what to do. Let me ring him. Oh, please – there must be some mistake!'

The woman in red approached the bed and leaned over it. Her white fingers, tipped with scarlet claws, stroked Sandra's hair.

'Oh no – there's no mistake, Mlle de Moncet.'

Sandra managed to get to her feet. 'Don't you dare touch me!' She shouted the words hysterically, and tried to push the strange woman away and run to the door. But an extraordinary violent blow sent her reeling back on the bed. Her head hit the wooden bedpost, and she burst into tears.

'There, don't cry,' whispered the woman in red, who had not lost her self-control for a single moment. 'You're lucky, after all. I'm sure we shall get on very well together – and as you'll soon find out, the Café Américain is the best house in all Casablanca.'

6

Out in the flower-planted patio, only the splashing of a fountain broke the afternoon calm. A faint heat haze hovered above the languid bodies of the three intrepid girls who had ventured out, well covered in suntan cream, to lie on loungers beside a lemon tree. The other girls were in their rooms off the gallery, sheltering from the heat of the sun behind closed doors. The woman in red sitting at a cane table under the gallery was playing patience. She turned up the King of Spades and put the card in the black column, all the time keeping an eye on the telephone at her feet. When it rang the woman did not jump.

'Yes? Good afternoon . . . yes, of course. We'll see you soon, then.'

She put the receiver down and turned up a seven.

'Katia, M. Ben Hasser will be here in an hour's time. He wants you,' she said in peremptory tones.

One of the three girls got off her lounger and made as if reluctantly for the closed doors. 'Okay, Ice, I'll go and get ready.'

Anya Calezza went back to her game of patience. Her close friends (not that there were many of them) could have told that she was waiting for someone from the way she was drawing on her cigarette holder. Also that the visitor was late. Everyone in Casablanca knew that Ice ruled her girls with a rod of iron, but those who knew her real name were few. A Maltese who had been living in Morocco for twenty years, she had almost lost trace of her origins herself. Nothing but the present concerned her – and today the present was not much to her taste. Slim Ferraci was one of those people who are never on time, and Ice, who regarded punctuality as a virtue, was getting impatient.

A little Arab girl wearing an apron and a white cap which scarcely confined her mass of hair timidly approached the woman in red, bent down and whispered something in her ear.

'Ah! Show him into my office, Zina.'

Mouse-like, the girl disappeared into the depths of the house. Ice rose, smoothing down her dress over her hips with a practised gesture. Unhurriedly, she turned towards the recption room, crossed the hall, which was restfully cool, and opened her office door. She entered a large, light room, sparsely furnished. A fat man with an affable expression on his face rose as she came in.

His white suit was crumpled, and a tarboosh was perched precariously on his head. A smile spread over his sweaty face as he raised Ice's hand to his lips. But his little green eyes, set off by his dark skin, deceived no one, least of all Ice. They were cold and cruel as a reptile's, and they said clearly who was master. Ice withstood that gaze without flinching.

'My dear, what heat!' breathed Ferraci, letting himself drop back into his chair. He mopped his brow with a folded handkerchief. 'Good for business, though, eh? The sun softens up hearts and bodies.'

Ice fitted a Benson and Hedges cigarette into her holder. 'Yes, Ferraci, we're not short of clients.'

'Good, good!' Impatiently, he swatted a fly that was buzzing around his head.

'I suppose you've come to see out latest acquisition?' inquired Ice, perching on a corner of her desk and crossing her long, black-stockinged legs.

'Yes, of course . . . the new girl.' Ferraci was staring at her thighs. 'Of course . . . '

Ice savoured her brief moment of revenge. Ferraci had wanted her ever since the start of their association over fifteen years earlier. After all, wasn't he the master here? Didn't he have the *droit de seigneur* over all the inmates of the establishment – and the madam who ran it? But for fifteen years Ice had lived up to her nickname.

'Okay.' Ferraci seemed to shake himself. 'Let's see the girl.'

Hips swaying, Ice walked over to the only picture in the room: a delicate engraving of a male nude. She carefully moved it aside to reveal a pane of glass looking into the red room. Ferraci went over to it and cast a glance at the place where Sandra had been imprisoned for the last four days.

Face distorted and streaming with tears, the girl was hammering on the door with all her might, unaware that the room was soundproofed and the mirror hanging above the bed showed every detail of her anguish.

'Hmm – the tearful type, but she looks as if she'll do,' said Ferraci. 'Why isn't she at work yet?'

Ice moved the picture back into place and went to her desk.

'Every fish must get used to its aquarium, Ferraci,' she said. 'And this one hasn't taken the measure of hers yet.'

Ferraci's right eyebrow rose in surprise. 'Can the heat be softening you up, my dear?'

'The fact is, she's not ready yet, Ferraci. Mallowan's tried her out in Paris already. I expect him here in two days' time.'

'Ah, well, we need a few restive fillies – and it wouldn't do for Mallowan to lose his touch, would it? I have every confidence in you, my dear . . . ' Ferraci rose, took Ice's hand again, and raised it to his lips. 'Two days – but no longer.'

His green gaze met Ice's eyes. Ferraci turned and, with surprising grace for so fat a man, made for the door.

When he had left Ice sighed, put another Benson and Hedges into her cigarette holder, and tried to convince herself yet again that working for a slimy rat meant nothing to her one way or the other.

He was a man of about forty, quite attractive, who looked like a businessman, wearing an immaculate alpaca suit. And there he was in her room. Sandra recognized him. She remembered the darkness of an archway, a penis thrust against her, the taste of shame. She was about to cry out, but the man put a hand over her mouth and pulled her towards him. Arms pinioned behind her back, Sandra felt as if she were held in a vice. She struggled, and the man held her all the more firmly. She realized that for now her only chance was to keep calm.

Sensing her docility, the man let her go.

'What do you want?' she asked, voice trembling. 'And who *are* you?'

'My name is Leslie Mallowan,' said the man, casually.

'And will you kindly tell me what I'm doing here?'

The man sat down in the red armchair, hitching his trousers up slightly around the knee, and crossed his legs gracefully.

'My dear Sandra – it seems to me you've had a week in which to work out the answer to *that!* If you haven't guessed yet – well, that's just too bad for you.' Mallowan uncrossed his legs and rose smoothly to his feet. 'As for what *I* want – that' simple,' he went on. 'I want you, my dear Sandra, that's all!'

'I don't understand,' she said, trying to steady her voice.

'Well, since you seem to want it all spelt out, we're going to have a repeat performance of our little interlude in Paris.'

Sandra cast him a horrified glance and retreated to the wall, her hands against the red velvet.

'No!' she whispered.

But in a moment he was on her, crushing her in his powerful arms and dragging her to the bed. Sandra struggled, tried to bite and scratch, but her pitiful resistance only made Mallowan smile.

'There – take it easy,' he murmured. 'I like a wildcat!'

He flattened her on the bedspread, immobilizing her legs and arms and pinning her there with his full weight.

'Now you'll show me what you can do!' Holding Sandra's wrists with one hand, he lifted her dress and tore off her briefs with the other.

'Let me go!' snarled Sandra, her eyes flashing with rage.

'In a minute – in a minute.'

Sandra raised her head and spat in her attacker's face. Unmoved, Mallowan smiled. He got his handkerchief out with his free hand and wiped his cheeks and forehead. Then he slowly put the handkerchief away, as if relishing what was about to happen in advance, and hit Sandra hard.

Her head went back against the bedpost. She uttered a miserable animal cry, and tears sprang from her eyes, running down her face. Mercilessly, Mallowan undid his trousers and brought out his erect penis. Pulling Sandra's head down to it he hissed, 'Suck it! And I'll kill you if you bite!'

Sandra was still weeping. Her mouth obstinately refused to open, and she was shaken by convulsive sobs. Mallowan took his victim's chin between thumb and forefinger, made sure his fingers had a good grip on her wet cheeks, and then pushed abruptly. With a moan of pain, Sandra opened her lips.

'Now!'

He thrust his penis into her wide-open mouth. Dazed, Sandra did not react. Mallowan tore the front of her dress open, exposing her breasts, and roughly manipulated them. Then he took one nipple and pinched it hard.

'You're going to suck me off, you dirty slut!'

Sandra's body was shaken by a violent spasm. Vanquished by the pain, she surrendered. Slowly, her lips began to move.

'That's better – that's good. Keep going.'

Blinded by tears and choked by her sobs, Sandra sucked the erect penis farther in. She wanted to go fast and get it over and done with. Mallowan grunted. Sandra could feel the pressure of his hands relax. He panted like a wild beast, and came in the girl's mouth. Yet she had the impression that he had never really lost control of himself for so much as a second.

'Swallow it, Sandra,' he ordered as he did his trousers up. She felt a violent surge of nausea rise in her throat.

Mallowan sketched a gesture towards one of her nipples.

With an effort. Sandra swallowed, and then fell back on the bed, burying her face in her hands. Her body was still shaken by convulsive spasms, but her tears had dried up.

'That'll do for today.'

Mallowan rose, smoothed down his jacket sleeves, and left the room. Sandra ran to the little bathroom and collapsed there with her head in the basin.

A week of torment. Sandra still would not accept what she now realized was inevitable. Her body rejected the idea. She was imprisoned in that red room, and Mallowan's visits were all that punctuated her time there. It seemed a long time, for she willingly allowed herself to drift into a state of lethargy, almost a coma. It was her only refuge. The very last thing she wanted to do was think, but beyond the mists she felt the trap closing in. Yesterday, she had not put up so much resistance to Mallowan's violent assault on her.

Deep in her abused body, she almost thought she felt an echo of pleasure reborn . . .

The door of her prison suddenly opened. Sandra did not even sit up. She knew the little Arab maid would put a tray on the table. She had not touched the food for the first few days. Then, despite herself, her appetite returned. She had once tried to make a dash for the door while the girl was busy setting out her meal, but when she found herself facing a gleaming razor blade, casually brandished by the little man in white who had met her at the airport, she gave up.

'Hullo. My name's Laure.'

Sandra started. Quickly, she sat up on the bed. It was not the little Arab maid, but a tall, blonde girl, supple and slender. Sandra could see her breasts through the fine white cotton djellabah she was wearing. Her erect nipples brushed against the fabric whenever she moved.

'Who are you?' said Sandra, timidly.

'I work here, like you,' said Laure, offering her hand. 'Come and get some fresh air out in the patio. It's still quite pleasant there this morning.'

Sandra shrank back against the bedhead.

'I do *not* work here!' she spat between her teeth.

She shot the girl a frenzied glance, and then burst into tears.

Laure sat down beside her, putting a hand on her shoulder. 'There now, have a good cry,' she said softly. 'You'll have forgotten all about it tomorrow! You'll get used to it, like the rest of us.'

Sandra raised her tear-filled eyes. 'Never!' she cried.

Laure shook her head. 'Come on, let's go into the patio,' she repeated in a faraway tone.

And she helped Sandra to take her first few steps outside her prison.

'*I* think you'd look better in deep pink,' said Lili. 'Here – try this on.'

Sandra slipped into the long, close-fitting, coral-coloured dress, and turned round in front of the mirror.

'Goodness, how lovely you look!' cried Mady, a plump, well-covered little brunette.

She fussed around Sandra, feeling her hair, rolling one auburn ringlet round her fingers.

'If only *I* had eyes like that! Mady went on. Suddenly she stopped, and then added, rapidly, 'Well, my dears, from now on we must face the fact that we have serious competition!'

The five girls around her chuckled. They sounded friendly.

Seeing herself in their eyes, Sandra felt good for the first time in days. She even found herself smiling. She had not been left alone for a moment since she left the prison of her room. The other girls flocked around her and petted her as if she were their child.

Laure got to her feet. 'Come along – time for bed, everyone, it's four o'clock. You'll have dark circles under your eyes tomorrow.'

Kind but firm, she shooed the girls out of the room she and Sandra were sharing, and off they went twittering like a flock of birds.

Laure undressed and got into bed. 'You should go to bed too, Sandra. You're starting work tomorrow.'

Standing by the window that looked out on the patio, Sandra shivered. Starting work tomorrow – work as a prostitute! Oh no, she cried silently to herself. When Mallowan had not re-appeared she thought the nightmare was over. The girls' warm friendliness and constant chatter were comforting, and helped her to make her peace with herself. She had almost forgotten what was to come.

'Laure,' she began. 'I want to ask you something.'

'Sandra, we've discussed this over and over again!' Laure sat up in bed, sounding annoyed. 'The Café Américain has its rules, and you must respect them like everyone else. I know what you're going to ask, and the answer is *no*!'

'But at least you *know* why you're here!' cried Sandra. She threw herself on the bed beside Laure. 'You chose the rules of this game! I didn't.'

'Yes . . . yes, I chose them.' Laure was looking into space.

'Laure, please!' Sandra persisted. 'You're the only one who's free to come and go as you like. Just one telephone call when you go out, that's all I'm asking . . . '

Laure sighed, and tried to escape Sandra's pleading eyes.

'All right, you win! I'll ring your Marc for you.'

'Oh, thank you!' Sandra threw her arms round the other girl's neck and kissed her affectionately. '*Now* I can go to bed!'

She undressed quickly and slipped into her own bed, beside Laure's.

'After all, it won't be so terrible. It only means making love to a man, doesn't it?'

Laure did not reply.

'Doesn't it?' Sandra's voice shook slightly.

'Yes, Sandra. Making love to a man – and Ice.'

7

'Well, my dear Nelson, here is the surprise I mentioned,' said Ice.

The man put his glass down on the coffee table in the reception room and looked up at Sandra. In the coral sheath dress, she was a dazzling sight. Her skilfully disarranged hair made a coppery halo round her face.

'Fabulous!' said Nelson Akkar, letting a sigh of amazement escape him.

Sandra sat down opposite him, unobtrusively taking stock. He was attractive. She wondered whether that was just chance, or whether all the girls were allowed an attractive man first time. His eyes dwelt on her, and the desire she saw in his face was familiar, almost reassuring. She crossed her legs provocatively, revealing the sweet curve of a thigh. Suddenly she was beginning to enjoy playing with the man who would be her first client. She knew he was a Brazilian businessman, and she had been told to speak English to him. Ice, cool as ever, had made her repeat her instructions as she dressed and put on her make-up under the madam's critical eye.

As she showed herself off to the man, a strange sensation came over Sandra. It was so long since she had made love – over a month, perhaps. Mallowan didn't count: she was trying to pretend he never existed.

Ice rose, like a *maître de ballet*. It was the signal for them to leave this room. All three of them went into a bedroom where Sandra had never been before. Ice's own room. She thought Nelson Akkar must be a very privileged client to be permitted to make love here in the lioness's den. Unless it was because Ice still distrusted her new girl; perhaps she preferred to be in her own quarters and felt she could manage Sandra better there.

'Come in, my dear Nelson,' said Ice, standing back to let the man go first.

The room was white and bare. Sandra was surprised. She had been expecting some palatial, Oriental, sinister spot that matched its owner. Instead, she found herself in a simple but comfortable room with a vast bed holding pride of place. Sandra thought, suddenly, that the woman was a mystery. They had hardly exchanged a word since her arrival at the Café Américain, and she told herself that perhaps she should revise her opinion of Ice. Then she remembered that she was supposed to be going to make love to Ice in a few minutes' time, and the blood froze in her veins. Suddenly she remembered May's warm, sweet flesh. She felt sure she could not bring herself to repeat that experience with the woman she regarded as her jailer.

Control yourself, Sandra, she told herself sternly. Whores aren't supposed to *get* pleasure, they're there to give it.

A professional to her fingertips, Ice was in charge of the whole scene. She helped Nelson off with his jacket. Her gestures were caressing and sure. Sandra felt rigid and frozen. You must pretend, she kept telling herself, you must pretend.

'Would you like to begin with Sandra?' asked Ice.

'By all means.' Nelson's smile was that of a connoisseur..

Sandra had not moved. She was standing by the door, and suddenly it seemed as though she couldn't make out what she was doing here. Ice came over and took her gently by the hand.

'Now, your turn, my dear,' she murmured.

But the pressure of her hand on Sandra's was a command.

Sandra started – and suddenly she decided she would make love to this man in a perfectly straightforward way, as if she had met him at some reception and chosen him as a lover.

Turning her back to the Brazilian, she asked coaxingly, 'Dear, would you undo my dress for me?'

A gleam of approval came into Ice's eyes. She was sure that all would go well now.

Nelson pulled Sandra's zip down, and the gauzy fabric of the dress fell at her feet. She was wearing delicate white lace underclothes. She turned to face the man and let him admire her for a few moments. Then her hands went round his neck and she kissed him.

Surprised by her passionate foreplay, the Brazilian gave a start – but Sandra's gentle tongue was having its effect, and when she let her hand slip between his thighs she could tell he already had an erection. Taking her time, she undressed him, and it was she who urged him towards the bed. Nelson Akkar seemed very much aroused. He exposed Sandra's breasts, stroked them, took the nipples in his mouth. When his fingers made their way between the silk of her panties and her equally silken skin, Sandra, her breath coming short, felt desire rise in her. She wanted this man – and she told herself that wasn't normal, she oughtn't to want him.

Ice had undressed too. Standing beside the bed, she watched the couple playing with each other. She knew her client would soon ask her to join in too. He liked women so much that he got even more pleasure from watching them caress each other than possessing them himself.

Sandra's breath was coming in gasps now. Her eyes closed, she was waiting for the man to take her. Still caressing her, Nelson looked at her with a fond, indulgent smile.

'Ice!' he said.

She came over, exchanging a glance of complicity with the Brazilian.

'Well – this *is* a surprise! I wouldn't have missed it for the world,' murmured Nelson, still caressing Sandra.

Ice bent over and picked up a long black box which was lying beside the bed. She opened it. It contained five dildoes of different shapes and materials. Examining them, she chose one which perfectly imitated the texture of a penis, and fastened it to her waist. She still had her suspender belt on.

Drowning in her pleasure, Sandra still had her eyes closed. The man's hand was stroking her swollen vulva. Suddenly, she felt a weight on her body. Her hips rose to meet the penis she guessed was coming in. She opened her eyes to look at her lover – and saw what had happened. Nelson Akkar had moved away, and it was Ice above her now. A look of panic came into Sandra's eyes, but Ice gave her no time to react. With one violent movement of her hips she penetrated Sandra.

Sandra's desire was stronger than her surprise. She let herself come. Vagina enfolding the dildo plunging into her, her haunches rose to meet the other woman's and she moaned aloud.

Sitting on the edge of the bed, Nelson Akkar was slowly caressing himself. His eyes were riveted to those two dark triangles of hair rising and falling rhythmically towards each other. The heavy perfume of the woman's hot bodies rose in the room. Crying out, Sandra came to orgasm. As if a signal had been given, Nelson got behind Ice and took her while she went on thrusting the dildo into Sandra. The more violent Sandra's orgasm seemed, the more uncontrolled Ice became herself. She hardly seemed to notice Nelson penetrating her.

Worn out, vaguely disgusted, but with her whole body relaxed, Sandra saw Ice's face drop its stern mask for the first time. The madam of the Café Américain seemed to have forgotten her client, her brothel, her way of life. Ice was smiling, with her eyes closed.

'I thought it would be better not to tell you too much beforehand. I was afraid you'd panic – but that's what she always does when a girl is starting. And it's always with Nelson. That way, she can get her own kicks and keep an eye on the girl at the same time.'

Laure gave Sandra a glass of barley water. Lying on her bed, Sandra was watching the flies circling on the ceiling.

'It's the best way to get the girl broken in, too," Laure added.

She opened the shutters. The hot afternoon air, laden with the scent of jasmine, flooded into the room. Laure turned to Sandra.

'Sandra, what's the matter? Tell me, do!'

'I couldn't care less about any of that, Laure, and you know it. There's only one thing I want to hear about.'

Laure lowered her eyes and turned away. She watched three flies circling silently in the hazy air outside the window. She bit her lower lip, and said abruptly, 'Well, I did call your husband.'

Sandra trembled.

'Yes?' she breathed.

'The number you gave me was discontinued . . . Sandra, I'm terribly sorry.'

One way of life is much the same as any other, Sandra told herself every morning, and after all, a whore's life is not so bad. She had become used to the slow passing of the hours, broken by the regular visits of the American who never took his chewing gum out, the Moroccan banker whose sole interest was in what lay at the base of her back, and the Frenchmen who had come to Casablanca for a convention of some kind and were out on the spree, making a party out of a group visit to the brothel. Sandra discovered the facts of life that her sheltered childhood at Ramboiullet and her experience as a diplomat's wife had never let her suspect: men do visit prostitutes regulary, and the most enthusiastic of a brothel's clients are not necessarily sexual misfits. She tried to lose herself in observing what went on around her, so as not to think of her own desperate situation, and to avoid asking herself the questions that preyed on her mind. Ice seemed to trust her now, thought not yet enough to send her to clients outside the brothel walls. But she knew she had learnt to give pleasure to her transient visitors – and sometimes she got it from them, too. On occasion her clients were pleasant and kind, and then she gave herself generously. Other clients were more demanding, sometimes even cruel, and they only got the minimum of her. But Sandra noticed that all of them, without exception, acted in a prostitute's arms as if they were at a psychoanalyst's: they abandoned all reserve and exposed their innermost thoughts without any shame.

In the female world where Sandra now found herself, men regressed to the status of children, to be coaxed, protected and supported.

If you came to think of it, Sandra told herself, the whore and the diplomat's wife were not so very far apart. All such women served men, some sexually, others as power objects. And sometimes Sandra came close to thinking that prostitutes, who got paid for their services and did an honest job of work, followed as honourable a profession as the diplomats' ladies. Sometimes, when she liked a client, she even found herself enjoying her work – and that did scare her.

Laure often tried to comfort her by saying, 'We all get to that point – even the toughest and most fastidious of us. You get used to the life after a while and settle down.' But Sandra did not want to settle down. As she got dressed, this particular evening, she was urging herself to struggle against her alarming ability to adapt. The resignation to her lot which had made her accept it was too easy. She *must* get out of here – if only to discover the reason for her presence in the place. She must talk to Marc. Marc. When she thought of him hatred blurred her mind. Part of her said he had deserted her. Maybe he had even set the trap for her himself. Yet another part of her couldn't help imagining her husband searching all over the world for her, moving heaven and earth to get her back.

'You know who's visiting us this evening?'

It was Mady who spoke, bursting into the room in a whirlwind of red and green taffeta.

'No, who?'

Without turning round, Sandra went on outlining her lips with russet-coloured lip pencil. She was used to Mady's spectacular entrances – the other girls seldom bothered with conventional courtesies.

'The whole American Embassy, my dear! What an evening – what a feather in Ice's cap! It's the first time *they've* been here! And isn't she just excited – you can hear her carrying on even this far away!'

Sandra listened. Sure enough, muffled shouts reached her ears, though the door was closed. There was a sound of china or glass breaking. The other girls must have taken refuge prudently in their rooms. It was poor Zina, the maid, who seemed to be the butt of Ice's anger. The madam of the Café Américain sounded even more terrifying when she spoke Arabic, a sweet but harsh language which could sting like a whip in her mouth.

'I'm ready,' said Sandra, rising to her feet. 'Come on, Mady, let's see what's going on.'

'You're crazy! I'm staying her till the Americans arrive.'

Sandra put her head on one side and smiled winningly at the little brunette. 'Coward! Come on, are you going to leave me to face her all alone?'

Mady looked sulky, and then burst into a ripple of laughter. She linked arms with Sandra, and the two of them made for the big reception room where the brothel's clients made their choices from among the girls.

The shouts grew louder as they approached the room. Pausing in the doorway, Sandra and Mady saw a curious scene: Ice was pacing around the little Arab maid like a Fury, cursing her volubly, while Zina, on all fours on the Bokhara carpet, was picking up broken fragments which had been a set of glasses only a little while before.

The two girls' arrival seemed to take Ice's mind off her anger.

'What are *you* doing here? Go back to your rooms and get ready!'

Mady, half-hiding behind Sandra, was about to retreat. But Sandra knelt down and began to help pick up the bits of glass.

'We're ready now, Ice,' she said calmly.

Ice remained motionless for several serconds, her breath taken away by such audacity. For a brief moment the two women's glances met defiantly. Then, to Sandra's great relief, Ice turned on her heel and marched off to her office.

Zina picked up the last bits of glass from the carpet and put them in a large bucket. She rose and hurried towards the hall, but at the last moment she turned back.

'Thank you!' she whispered rapidly. Then she disappeared towards the kitchen.

Mady let out a long sigh. 'Wow!'

'Oh, Mady, if only you could see yourself!' cried Sandra, laughing. 'Anyone would think you'd just swallowed a goldfish bowl, fish and all!'

At nine o'clock the girls were all assembled in the drawing room. There were twelve of them. They were gathered in small groups, talking quietly as they sipped Coca Cola or barley water. The girls did not drink alcohol themselves: that privilege was reserved for clients, who sometimes turned up with a case of champagne, whisky or gin. Ice sat enthroned in her cane peacock chair, which rose in a high frame behind her head. She had not alluded to the incident when Sandra stood up to her again, but by now Sandra knew Ice well enough to be sure there would be retribution. There always was, even if it was some time coming. The Lady in Red never forgot.

The whole first part of the evening had been booked by the American Embassy. One of the Embassy staff, a regular client at the Café Américain, had decided to show his friends and colleagues how to have a good time in Casablanca. This was good business for Ice, and the girls liked it too. Group evenings were pleasanter and more relaxed, and demanded less effort on their part.

When the six men arrived Ice hurried to meet them. John Gavin, the regular client, performed the introductions. He "knew" all the girls – in the Biblical sense of the word. Sandra told herself he must have given his friends a little verbal sketch of each of them, and amused herself for a moment wondering what he had said about *her*.

A pretence of conversation began. Ice was talking about the international situation, while Zina served the men's drinks. The girls talked, showed their legs, displayed their charms. Sandra was watching it all, and suddenly she had the curious sensation of being on the wrong side of the barrier. After all, it was not so very long since she had been in the rooms of an embassy with these men, or men like them. Free, perhaps even happy.

A man approached her. He was tall, dark and blue-eyed. He made her a little bow.

'May I introduce myself? I'm Philip Dern. I'd like to make love to you.'

Still bowing, he cast Sandra a mischievous and inquiring glance.

Sandra burst into a ripple of clear laughter. 'I'm always surprised by the frankness of Americans – *and* their impatience!'

'Oh, I see I've met an expert!' he said quizzically. 'I can tell you're cut out for an anthropologist – I've been watching you watch all of *us!*'

'Is that why you picked me?'

Philip Dern's eyes travelled over Sandra's breasts, her waist, down her legs.

'Well, yes – and for one or two other reasons as well!'

Sandra laughed again. She thought him amusing. He was not really handsome, but he had the charm of self-assurance.

'Very well,' she said, 'let's be the first, shall we?'

She rose and walked towards the gallery which led to the girls' rooms.

The others looked at them, smiling.

'There goes Dern, always in a hurry!' John Gavin called. 'Take your time, old friend, it's all been paid for!' he added, guffawing.

Dern had joined Sandra and was now walking beside her. 'I apologize for that. I've always thought Gavin rather vulgar.'

'Oh, don't let it bother you,' said Sandra, rather drily. 'I mean, that's what we're here for – me and the other girls.'

Philip Dern did not reply. They entered Sandra's room.

'Any preferences?' she asked casually, beginning to undo the front of her dress.

'Yes – I'd like you to keep your clothes on.'

'Anything you say,' she replied with a trace of irony in her voice.

Why did the man suddenly make her feel so angry? Because he brought back her past too vividly? She didn't want to know the answer. She lay down on her bed. Obviously Philip Dern was the masterful sort and wanted to take the initiative.

Silently, the man sat down beside her and slowly undressed her, enjoying each move he made for itself as much as for the beauties it revealed. Sandra watched Dern's hands brush her body, play with her breasts, stroke her stomach and the dark triangle between her thighs.

'Stand up. I want to look at you.'

His voice was husky, and desire made him tremble slightly.

As usual, Sandra noticed the precise moment when her client felt her become his – a docile object. She tried to imagine the sensation of power which a man must feel with a prostitute, a woman paid to obey his slightest whim. A sensation of power, yes – but of total vulnerability too. Which was really dominating the other in the sensual game?

She rose and walked gracefully up and down the room, her breasts rising and falling in time to her footsteps. She stopped very close to Dern's face. He buried his head between Sandra's breasts, and then took her.

Philip Dern made love vigorously and tenderly. As if he were making love to a *real* woman, Sandra thought. She ought to let herself go, but she couldn't. She ought to have an orgasm (like many men, she sensed, he'd do anything for that), but still she couldn't. And when she felt he was about to ejaculate, tears began to run down her cheeks.

Philip Dern let out a brief cry and then collapsed on Sandra's body. Forgetting all about her, he enjoyed the intensity of his orgasm to the full. When he came back to reality he saw Sandra's distorted face. She was trying to control her tears, but could not manage to.

'Say – what's wrong? Did I hurt you?'

Gently, he stroked her face. She sobbed even harder, and he sat up, concerned.

'Would you like me to call someone? What ought I to do?'

He was beginning to panic, and Sandra, making a great effort, at last managed to choke back her tears.

'It – it's all right," she gulped. 'Only my nerves.' Then, sitting up bravely, she added, 'Don't worry. I'll be fine now.'

'Well, you really had me scared,' said Dern, sitting down on the bed again. 'Listen, what's your name?'

'Sandra.' He stroked her face again, and then began to get dressed. Suddenly he seemed ill at ease. 'How do I . . . what do I do about . . . ?'

'The fee? That's Ice's business. Anyway, didn't your friend say it was all paid for?'

'Yes. Sure. Sorry, I'm not used to this – this sort of . . . '

Sandra said nothing, leaving him to extricate himself from his own embarrassment. He flushed red as he put his tie on. When he was ready he bent down to her, planted a chaste kiss on her cheek, and went to the door. He turned the handle, and then stopped and looked at her.

'Tell me, Sandra, just what *is* a girl like you doing in this sort of place? You're worth better than this.'

She looked at him, startled, and then burst into shrill laughter. He hurried away without closing the door behind him.

8

She had made up her mind, and nothing would make her change it now. Everything was fixed for six o'clock. It had taken her three days to win Laure over, two more for them to lay their plans and wait for the right moment.

Sandra put on the blonde wig. Laure was pacing around the room, wringing her hands.

'But even if you *do* get to the airport, then what will you do, without money or a passport?'

'I'll manage.'

Sandra finished doing up the dress Laure had given her. It was rather big for her, but it would be all right if she belted it in.

'Sandra, you're crazy. You don't realize what you're risking.'

Sandra suddenly turned to face her. 'I just can't stand it here any more, Laure. Don't you understand? Anyway, it's too late for me to draw back now.'

Laure bit her lip, sat down in the armchair and rose again at once. Picking up her handbag, she searched about in it for something, and then seemed to be doing the same with Sandra's, stuffing something into it.

'Here,' she said afterwards. 'It's not a lot, but it may help.'

She was holding out a wad of green banknotes.

'Oh, Laure, no – keep your money! I can't take it from you.'

But Laure forced the dollar notes into Sandra's hand.

'Don't argue! It's only a hundred. You can give them back when we meet again.'

Sandra lowered her eyes, and then bent down to kiss Laure's cheek. Laure gave herself a little shake and looked at her watch.

'Come on, then – it's nearly six. Try not to hurt me too much!'

'But I'm not really going to hit you! Tying you up will do.'

'No, it has to look good. If they suspect anything, I'll be in real trouble.'

'I suppose you're right. But I don't like it. Let me tie you up first.'

Laure lay down on the bed, and Sandra tied her hands and feet with the belts of both their dressing gowns.

'Now the gag.'

Sandra tied a red scarf round her friend's mouth. Then she straightened up and looked around her. 'What on earth can I hit you with? The lamp? No, that might cut your head open. That belt, perhaps – yes, that might do.'

She picked up a heavy black leather belt and came over to Laure.

'Are you all right like that? Not too uncomfortable?'

'Mmmm.' Laure was shifting restlessly, showing signs of impatience.

'All right, all right, I'm going.' She bent down to her victim and kissed her forehead. 'Thank you, Laure,' she whispered.

Then she raised the belt, shut her eyes, and brought it down with all her might on Laure's head. The girl's moan was muffled by the gag. Her body arched up, and then went limp.

'Oh, Laure – I'm so sorry!'

Sandra put on her friend's cape, pulling the hood over her blonde wig and as far as possible round her face. She put several things in her bag: the dollars, the map of the area Laure had drawn her, and a tiny 6.35 with no ammunition in it, which Laure had kept carefully hidden at the bottom of a drawer.

Sandra made for the door, and turned for a last look at the body stretched on the bed. Then she drew a deep breath and left the room. The hardest part was going to be tricking the guard at the outside door. Mario was cunning, and she knew from experience that he wouldn't hesitate to use his razor blade. Sandra tiptoed along the gallery. At this time of day, luckily, most of the girls were in their rooms getting ready for the evening. She reached the big glazed door of the drawing room, and slipped into the recess of the doorway. Then she heard voices. She immediately flattened herself against the wall. Ice had just entered the drawing room, barring her way out through it to the hall!

Sandra was gasping, unable to control her breathing. Ice was talking to Zina, the little maid. She seemed to be going to stay in the drawing room.

Sandra was in despair. Suppose her plan were to fail simply because Ice had chosen to indulge in her favourite occupation of bawling out the little Arab girl once again? She sounded as if she planned to go on and on!

Sandra went weak at the knees. She clung to the glazed door, and in her panic she made the latch rattle as she leaned on it.

'What's going on out there? Go and see what it is, Zina!'

Unable to move, Sandra stayed close to the wall. She knew she ought to run, to take refuge in one of the rooms opening off the gallery, but her legs simply would not carry her. She heard Zina's footsteps approaching the door. The little maid came out into the gallery, turning her head to left and then to right. When she saw Sandra she jumped, but made no sound. Her black eyes met Sandra's violet gaze. Sandra still had not moved.

Quickly, the little maid turned and went back into the drawing room. Closing her eyes, Sandra waited like a condemned man expecting to hear the whistle of the guillotine blade coming down.

'It's nothing, madame. Only the cat.'

'Dirty creature!; snapped Ice. 'I told Lili to keep it in her room! Very well – you come to the kitchen with me.'

Sandra felt her lungs emptying like two deflated balloons.

She waited for several seconds, offering up silent thanks to little Zina, to make sure the two women really had left the room. For a moment she wondered whether the girl had come to her aid out of affection for herself or hatred for Ice.

Then her sense of urgency returned. She hurried through the drawing room and out into the hall.

Pulling the hood down even farther over her eyes, Sandra adjusted her clothes and walked to the doorway with a firm tread. When she emerged at the top of the flight of steps a kind of intoxication came over her. She did not feel frightened any more. Mario was sitting on a garden chair reading a magazine. She marched boldly past him as he reluctantly looked up from it.

'Good evening, Mario,' she said, trying to imitate her friend's contralto voice.

'Oh, it's you, Laure,' said the little man in nasal tones. 'Ben Ali Gacem again? He's a lucky fellow, eh?'

'If you say so, Mario!'

She approached the steps leading to the garden and slowly began to go down them. Mario looked at her, slightly surprised, then shrugged his shoulders and returned to his magazine.

Sandra counted the steps. Only three more to the garden gate. Keep calm, Alexandra, she told herself. She closed the gate after her – it shut with a mournful squeal – and found herself out in the Boulevard de la Liberté. She turned left, as Laure had told her to do. For the moment she must go her friend's usual way to the Rue de Marseille, and above all she must not run.

When she reached the corner Sandra began trembling all over. She leaned against the wall. A taxi came past, and she hailed it.

'The airport, quick!'

Her heartbeat was having difficulty in recovering its normal rhythm. She still couldn't believe that she had actually escaped her prison – that she was free to go wherever she liked. With the money her friend had given her, and the little she had earned from her "work", she might have enough to buy an air ticket. Not a ticket to Paris, perhaps, but for the moment the main thing was to put as much distance as possible between herself and Casablanca. She looked at the back of the taxi driver's neck. It was so good to see an ordinary human being: a man who didn't want anything of her.

On the terrace, Mario found he had lost interest in the adventures of the strip cartoon hero in his magazine. Something in Laure's bearing had bothered him, though he could not say just what. He stroked his chin, and then suddenly rose and went back into the Café Américain.

Sandra was beginning to relax at last. The taxi had just left the outskirts of the city and was driving along the road to the airport. Another few minutes, and she could believe she was really free. She sank back in her seat, leaning her head against it and shutting her eyes. Immediately, a face rose behind her closed eyelids. Marc. She opened her eyes at once to banish the disturbing image. One problem at a time. That particular problem would have to wait a while for its solution.

Her taxi stopped outside the rectangular airport building. Sandra paid the fare and made for the glazed entrance. She glanced round the big hall with its rows of desks. Several travellers in a hurry were making for the departure gates. An Arab in a caftan passed her, pushing a litter bin mounted on wheels and carrying a broom. He casually swept up a few cigarette ends and an old newspaper. A Moroccan policeman was standing beside a panel of glass.

Suddenly out of breath, for no real reason, Sandra went over to the Air Morocco desk. After a brief conversation she found that there was a plane leaving for Lisbon in an hour's time. There was one empty seat, and she had just enough to pay for a ticket.

An hour to kill. An hour of suspense. She decided to have a coffee in the little cafeteria. Once in Lisbon she would go to the French Consulate, and they would help her get back to Paris.

In the Café Américain, the horrified Mario was looking at Laure's limp body on the bed. Without a moment's hesitation, he went back to the hall.

'You seem to be in a hurry, Mario,' said Ice.

'The bird's flown! I'm going to get her back.'

'*What?* What are you talking about?'

'Sandra. She went out instead of Laure.'

'How . . . ?'

'No time to tell you now – I'll soon be back.'

He hurried away.

'The little fool,' hissed Ice, between her teeth. 'That's all I need! Why did she have to run away? And this evening, of all times! Zina! *Zina!*'

Sandra had already drunk two cups of coffee. Calm down, she told herself, it will all be all right. Mario didn't recognize you. You'll soon be boarding that plane. She looked at her watch. In five minutes' time they would be summoning passengers to the departure gate. Only five minutes. Her hands were trembling, and she didn't even try to stop them.

Mario had taken Ice's Mercedes. He drove headlong through the city, crashing red lights, disregarding rights of way. His tyres screeched on the tarmac. Automatically, he regularly wiped away the beads of perspiration which stood out on his forehead.

'Will all passengers for Lisbon kindly go to Gate Number 3 to board their plane immediately? *Los viajeros . . .* '

Sandra rose at once and hurried to the barrier, where she came up against the Customs desk. Good God – she had completely forgotten she had no passport! She looked round in panic. There was nothing for it, you had to go through Customs to reach the departure gates.

A vast weariness suddenly descended upon her. All that effort for nothing! She couldn't leave. The plane for Lisbon would take off without her. In despair, she let herself fall on one of the upholstered seats. She dropped her handbag – its contents spilled on the floor – and raised a hand to her forehead. She no longer even had the strength to pick her things up.

A woman came over and knelt down beside her. An elegant European woman: kind-hearted, too. 'Don't you feel well, mademoiselle?' she asked.

'It's nothing. I'll be all right,' murmured Sandra in an expressionless voice.

The woman was starting to gather Sandra's things up and put them back in her bag.

'Please don't bother,' said Sandra.

'Oh, it's no trouble!' The woman smiled warmly at her. :There you are! I think that's everything. Oh no, wait a minute – your passport!'

'My passport?' Sandra almost shouted.

'Yes – here.' Looking rather surprised, the woman held out a little document with a blue plastic cover. Sandra automatically took it and opened it at the first page. Laure Vergnault, born 25th September . . . Without warning, tears rose to her eyes, and she got to her feet, clutching the passport convulsively.

'Thank you – oh, *thank* you!' she cried to the woman, who might well be regretting her kind gesture by now.

Feeling a surge of gratitude towards Laure, who had risked her life and perhaps her own eventual liberty for her, Sandra flew to the Customs desk and passed through easily. In the blonde wig, she looked quite like Laure, and the weary Customs officer was certainly taken in.

Sandra hurried down a long, grey corridor. All the other passengers must be in the aircraft by now. She was the last. A faint sense of uneasiness made her hurry even more. The empty corridor seemed to be going on for ever.

The footsteps came as if out of nowhere. They were irregular, echoing on the smooth floor-covering. Sandra suddenly felt as if she was drowning. She dared not turn round. The steps came closer. She began to run. Her pursuer was closing in on her.

Sandra's breathing came noisily. Just a little farther. She could already see the narrow ramp leading straight into the plane at the end of the corridor. Just a little farther . . .

A hand came down on her shoulder. An iron fist forced her round. The blade in Mario's hand flashed with rainbow light.

In a split second, all feeling left Sandra. She was nothing but a soft, warm victim, a rabbit with its bloody neck crushed in the spaniel's jaws. Hunter and hunted, they went back down the corridor. When Mario turned the key in the ignition, they still had not exchanged a word.

Ice was pacing nervously up and down the drawing room. The bell rang, and Zina started for the hall to answer it.

'No, I'll go myself,' said Ice, hurrying out. It's too soon for Mario to be back yet, she was thinking, so it must be *him*.

She showed her visitor in and led him to her office in silence.

'Well, good evening, Ice,' said the man, when the door had closed behind them.

'Good evening – listen, she's made a break for it, but Mario is after her, and he shouldn't be long.'

She had spoken very fast, without pausing for breath.

The man frowned slightly and then bared his teeth in a smile which did not reach his green eyes.

'Excellent!' he said. 'Excellent!' He sat down in the upholstered armchair opposite Ice's desk, and lit a cigarette.

'Excellent,' he repeated thoughtfully. 'Though ideally she should have had more than two months . . . '

She was not thinking, she was not expecting anything any more, she was incapable of feeling. She did not even notice that she was trembling all over with exhaustion. By the time Mario stopped the Mercedes outside the Café Américain, life had no past and no future so far as Sandra was concerned. Everything inside her had simply stopped.

Obedient and shivering, she got out of the car, climbed the steps to the door, and re-entered the place she had tried to leave an hour or so earlier. Now she would have to face Ice, but even that prospect could not rouse her from her apathy. She went to the office of the Lady in Red of her own accord. Like a faithful sheepdog, Mario followed her all along the corridor, then went ahead of her and opened the door. With a jerk of his head, he told her to go in. Sandra crossed the threshold, and the door closed after her. The fly was in the red spider's web.

Suddenly startled, she raised her head. The room was empty. Ice had decided to make her wait. Her punishment was beginning.

Someone in the armchair moved, catching her eye. A man got to his feet and came slowly towards her.

'I've been waiting for you, Sandra.'

'Marc!'

She thought she had screamed his name, but no sound at all came out of her mouth.

9

The plane touched down on the runway. The undercarriage bumped gently along, hissing slightly, and the economy class passengers clapped, applauding Captain Rivière for bringing the Air Morocco Boeing down at Orly Airport so skilfully. It was a habit Sandra hated – it seemed to turn the plane into a circus arena and the pilot into a performing monkey. Some people seemed to find playing with death more amusing than sexual games . . .

'You seem melancholy, Sandra.'

Marc had already unfastened his safety belt and was getting ready to leave his seat. He did not expect an answer. Sandra had refused to speak to him ever since their rapid departure from the Café Américain. He had not pressed her. He knew she would listen more easily to what he had to say in the comfort and intimacy of their apartment.

He left Sandra while he went to fetch his car from the parking area. Shivering in her thin dress, she waited, motionless, by the automatic doors. When Marc drew up beside her he got out to open the car door for her, and almost had to push her into the vehicle.

The BMW drove to Paris fast. Sandra tried to suppress the rage she felt rising within her. She decided not to talk, to let *him* try explaining, hear him entangle himself. She wouldn't say anything; she knew that if she opened her mouth nothing but a howl would emerge. As if in a dream, she saw herself in Ice's office again, rooted to the ground like a statue.

'Come on, we're leaving,' Marc had said.

And she had not seen any of them again: not the madam herself, or Laure, or Mario. She had simply walked to the door and out. A bitter taste came into her mouth when she thought of the hours of distress her own wretched attempt at escape had cost her.

The car took the south circulating Périphérique. Marc came off it at the Porte d'Auteuil, and drove along the Rue d'Auteuil to the Avenue Théophile-Gautier. He stopped outside a modern apartment building with a smooth glass façade. Sandra showed no surprise at all when he entered the hallway of the building, or when he stopped outside a heavy teak door on the fourth floor. He turned the key in the lock. 'Our apartment, Sandra,' he said.

She walked into a large white entrance hall. Ahead lay a spacious modern double drawing room, decorated in simple and excellent taste. Sandra noticed none of these details. She went straight to the sofa and sank on to it.

Marc made a small gesture of annoyance, which he quickly suppressed. This was going to be a difficult game to play, and he was not at all sure of winning it. He must go carefully.

He went over to Sandra, sat down beside her and tried to take her hand. She abruptly freed herself.

'Sandra . . . '

He hesitated, tried to look into her eyes, and then began again, firmly. 'Sandra, I know you must be expecting an explanation, and I've every intention of giving you one. I can assure you it will be adequate for what you've been through.'

She turned to him, hatred in her eyes, but he went steadily on.

'We're both worn out. Now look, why don't we make a bargain? You relax, take a bath, change, try to feel more like yourself. Meanwhile I'll fix some kind of dinner, and after we've eaten we'll talk like two adult people. What do you say?'

Sandra looked at him blankly.

'Have you *any* idea what you're asking?' she cried.

Pupils dilated, nostrils quivering, she was ready to spring at him – but there was nothing but tenderness, she saw, in the eyes resting on her.

She was under too much strain; she couldn't help it. Hysteria came welling up in her. She began to sob convulsively, hammering at the sofa cushions, stuffing her hands into her mouth to keep from screaming. She was cleansing herself of those two months when he had been using her. Absorbed in her grief, she did not see Marc rise and walk to the bedroom.

A little later he came back, picked her up in his arms and carried her into the bathroom. He gently undressed her and plunged her into a warm, scented bath. Docile as a child, she let him massage her back and the nape of her neck.

'Relax, Sandra,' he murmured.

Then he wrapped her in a big, warm towel, dried her, and put her to bed in the double bed. He dropped a kiss on her forehead and left the room in silence. By the time he closed the door, Sandra was asleep.

Only the chink of ice cubes in his glass disturbed the silence of the apartment. Seated in one of the drawing room armchairs by the big bay window, Marc was drinking his third gin. He had been sitting there for hours, looking at the lights of Paris reflected in the Seine.

Daylight woke Sandra. For a few seconds she did not know where she was. Then she remembered the events of the previous day, and sat up abruptly. The other side of the bed was empty. With a sigh of relief, she put on the green wrapper she saw thrown over a chair, and walked round the apartment, exploring it like a cat. In the kitchen, she made coffee and found what she needed for toast and scrambled eggs.

Marc had fallen asleep in his chair, fully dressed, his head on one shoulder. His glass had fallen to the floor. Sleep smoothed all the harshness from his face. When he was relaxed like that, she thought, he looked like some fair-haired child out of a fairy tale – Hansel lost in the forest, perhaps.

'Marc.'

Dressed and refreshed they were facing each other again. Sandra was quite calm now. She was the first to speak.

'Marc, I don't want to stay in this place. Let's go out.'

He smiled again, and repressed an affectionate gesture which she might have misunderstood.

'All right. Where do you want to go?'

'I don't know – a park, maybe?'

They went walking down the pathways of the Jardin des Plantes, still deserted at this hour of the morning, between papyrus reeds and dendrobiums.

'Sandra,' Marc began, hesitantly, 'there are a great many things in my life I've never been able to tell you about. However you judge me and what I've done, the way I've behaved, I want you to know that I love you . . . that I've always loved you.'

He tried to meet her eyes, but she avoided his glance.

'I'm listening, Marc.'

He took a deep breath and plunged in.

'It all began a long time ago – before I even met you. I was the son of a distinguished family, a diplomat with a promising future. When I had finished my studies and met James, we dreamed of great missions, journeys abroad . . . '

James. Sandra thought she had almost forgotten his name. She said nothing, but realized, wrily, that her memory of him was still painful.

'Well, let's just say we had a very romantic idea of our chosen profession. When we got to know your father he soon brought us down to earth. He took us under his wing, guided us through the diplomatic maze, introduced us to his influential friends . . . '

They were passing the zoo, which was still closed. They heard the cries of birds, and a trumpeting noise vibrating through the chilly air. Sandra wondered what Marc was driving at, but decided not to interrupt.

'It was then we really began to understand what we were getting into – what sort of job we'd chosen. You know, diplomacy is a curious career, Sandra: a contradictory profession, made up of communication and silence, futile chatter and well-kept secrets.'

He stopped for a moment, looked down, and then went on walking. They were approaching the vivarium.

'One meets some strange people,' Marc continued. 'And one sees and hears many things. All sorts and conditions of people elbow each other in an embassy, and the border between our diplomacy and intelligence work can be very hazy. Your father's friends . . . '

Sandra thought she could hear the hum of millions of insects in the humid obscurity of the big vivarium. 'What are you trying to tell me, Marc?' she interrupted. 'Why do you keep talking about my father? And just what has all this got to do with the fact that you kept me shut up in a brothel in Casablanca for two months?'

She had sworn to herself that she would not raise her voice again, but she felt that Marc was dragging her into quicksands from which she would not be able to free herself.

'Sandra, the service of the State sometimes takes devious ways. There was a certain project on which your father's friends had been working for a long time. They gave James and myself the job of putting the idea into practice. James had prepared a file – a file on you.'

'James? Why bring James into it again?' Sandra burst out. 'Marc, can't you leave James out of this and tell me plainly what it's all about?'

'Sandra, I've always wanted to share my life with you – my *whole* life. and that's why I built this whole project round you when your father's friends entrusted the delicate mission to me. That's why Casablanca was necessary. Before you'd been through that experience we didn't have a chance – you'd certainly have thought I was mad! Now we *may* have a chance.'

In its cage, a yellow snake coiled lazily around an artificial tree stump. Sandra began to see a pattern, through all he had left unsaid. It was like seeing a water-colour made up of thousands of tiny dots which combine to form a picture.

'And it didn't bother you to make me do that? It wouldn't bother you to think of your wife as a whore and a spy.'

She had raised her voice again. He came closer to her and took her arm, but she lowered her head and turned away.

'Sandra, I love you. Love doesn't mean possession, it means freedom. None of what I've told you over these last four years was untrue. I love to see you offered to others and know you're really mine.'

He took her chin in his hand and raised her head. His mouth brushed her cheek, following the track of a tear down to the corner of her lips.

'Today,' he said softly, 'you hold my career in your hands – the work of the last six years. I've staked everything on you, Sandra. I need you. If you refuse – well, my project's ruined.'

The bird-eating spider was waiting, silent in its glass case, squatting behind a piece of bark. The moment its prey moved, its eight hairy feet would go into action.

'I . . . I'll have to think about it,' Sandra said at last.

10

It must have been for that she agreed – for that moment of delicious triumph.

Marc did not understand, when she wanted to take him off to Morocco.

'But why do you want to go back there, Sandra? The place is nothing to do with us now.'

'This is very important, Marc. You *did* tell me Ice couldn't refuse you anything?'

'Yes, I did, but . . . '

'Then let's go! Now!'

When their hired green Ford stopped outside the Café Américain, Sandra could not suppress a shudder. She could never have foreseen that she would be back in this hateful place so soon.

She bore herself proudly as she entered her former prison. Obedient but puzzled, Marc followed her.

Zina, the little Arab maid, showed them into the drawing room. Nothing had changed in this room inhabited by women, but intended for men. There was still a heavy odour in the air: a mixture of jasmine, alcohol and perspiration. To Sandra, it was the smell of lust.

Ice had been told they were coming. Renan had phoned her from Paris to say so, and the news did not seem to have pleased her.

At last, she appeared in the drawing room, dressed in red, silent and aloof. She stood in the middle of the room, eyes slightly narrowed, waiting. Not at all flustered by this glacial reception, Sandra immediately went on the offensive.

'Will you call Laure, please?' she said briskly.

'But . . . '

Ice tried to protest, but a discreet signal from Marc told her to do as Sandra said. Nostrils quivering, she called Zina and gave her orders in a hoarse voice like the snarl of an animal.

A few moments later Laure entered the room, more blonde and cool even than Sandra remembered her. She stood motionless for several seconds, eyes wide, and then ran to her friend.

'Sandra! You, here? They found you again, didn't they?'

Sandra smiled, and the two women clung together in a long embrace. Laure was crying silently.

After a while Sandra freed herself, gently pushing Laure away and holding her at arm's length. 'Laure,' she asked, directly, 'would you like to come to Paris and work for me? I need you.'

Laure looked round, incredulous. Marc's amused smile and Ice's rigid mask were enough to convince her she was not dreaming.

'Oh yes, Sandra,' she replied. Then, in a clear voice, looking at Ice. 'Without any regrets at all!'

Next, Sandra turned to Zina, who had remained standing by the doorway, overlooked in the general confusion.

'What about you, Zina? Would *you* like to come to Paris with me?'

The little Arab girl nodded her head very fast, never taking her eyes off Ice – as if she expected to see her leap at her with all her claws out.

Sandra put her arms round the two women's shoulders and led them to the door. 'We're leaving at once. Ice will see that your things are sent on.'

And she left the Café Américain without a glance behind her.

Marc gave Ice a small, apologetic shrug of the shoulders and said, 'Send the bill to me,' before following the other three.

In the plane, they laughed like schoolgirls relishing a trick they had played on their teacher. But once back in

Paris they soon sobered down. Sandra had given her word, and now she must get down to work.

This evening, as she walked through the silent corridors of that very exclusive establishment on the Rue des Licornes, whose inmates at present numbered ten girls, Sandra felt a surge of gratitude towards the faithful Laure. Competent Laure who, thanks to her expert knowledge of the profession, had been endlessly patient, and had guided, helped and advised Sandra all through these last six months. Laure, her right hand, almost her other self!

First, they had to find a suitable building. They had seen dozens of places before coming upon this little jewel of a house in the heart of the seventh arrondissement. Laure had picked the domestic staff; Marc had provided everything necessary to do the place up. Like some great mythical ship, the Unicorn, as it was to be called, was beginning to spread its sails. All it needed now was the crew.

Sandra stopped on the first-floor landing.

Like being inside a luscious mandarin orange, she thought, stroking the deep orange velvet that covered the walls. She sat on the little beige sofa facing the staircase and looked around her. Behind closed doors lay ten of the wonders of the world. Sandra breathed a sigh of satisfaction. It had taken time to find ten girls who were bold, discreet, efficient – and crazy enough to accept the deal she put to them. Once again, Laure had been invaluable. It was now, too, that she learned to value Marc's competence, and the extent of the means he had at his disposal.

Sandra had interviewed dozens of potential candidates, travelling from continent to continent. Making good use of her contacts in diplomatic circles, thanks to Marc, she managed to open many supposedly impassable doors.

She met Maya in Cairo. Maya, an immensely tall, proud black girl, was an Ethiopian who had worked as a callgirl in London and then became the mistress of an English diplomat who was posted to Egypt. She threw it all up to take the job Sandra was offering.

In Rio, Sandra found Maria and Fedora, one from Brazil and the other from Argentina, in a *de luxe* establishment run by an American woman. She paid a very large sum to buy them out of their contracts.

She came away from Johannesburg with Toni, beautiful, blonde, and the daughter of the Dutch vice-consul.

In Dubai, she found Bettina, a go-getting German girl who meant to make a fortune out of the oil-rich sheikhs. The lovely Teutonic adventuress had also introduced Sandra to Ingrid, a former callgirl, now a Los Angeles model.

A friend of Laure's had sent them Kazuko and Shanah.

Finally, in New York, she met Jill the American girl, and Anci the Hungarian, employing their talents as dancers in a Broadway night club.

Tonight, the ten girls were sensibly getting a good night's rest. They were an essential part of the project, all ten making up a single unit, like the ten sections of some cosmopolitan orange. They had been given a very special training, as had Sandra and Laure. Psychologists, sexologists and intelligence experts had all played their part in making cool, detached observers out of these practitioners of the art of love.

Sandra rose. A door had just closed on the second floor, where she had her own three private rooms. Their walls were covered in peach silk. Laure's gone to bed, thought Sandra, pleased to feel she was alone here in the middle of the night. Soon she would go back to her rooms – the queen bee's cell, the only place in the building that the technicians had left untouched. There was not a single electronic gadget in her three rooms. Sandra preferred human voyeurism to the mechanical kind.

She went down into the red hall again. The hall mirrors showed her her own reflection repeated to infinity. Tomorrow you will shine, Sandra, they seemed to be saying. Like a little girl impressed by such grandeur, she sat down on the bottom step of the stairs, elbows resting on her knees. She knew the note of the doorbell, knew how her clients' footsteps would sound, echoing sharply as they walked over the marble flags. Gisele and Corinne would let them in, take their coats, show them into the big drawing rooms.

Sandra felt a sudden breath of cold air on her face – as if a ghost had slipped into the house, closing the door silently behind it. She rose and went into the garnet-red drawing room on the right.

She did not switch on the lights in the crystal chandeliers. In the dimness, her hand stroked the backs of the big sofas, covered with fuchsia chintz, and rested on the black grand piano, which looked like some pre-historic monster. She went over to the nearest of the three tall windows and moved the white net curtains aside. All was still, out in the little courtyard. Marc would not be back until a good deal later.

Sandra had wanted the two big reception rooms furnished in different styles. The white drawing room was all leather and steel, but despite her taste for the modern Sandra felt more at ease in the softer world of this room. It conjured up the fragrance of balls in bygone days, the sweetness of amber liquids, the swaying of tulle skirts.

She sat at the piano, slowly picking out the first notes of *A Foggy Day in London Town*. She was not sure why Gershwin's music should bring back images of the past, a memory of James's face – a memory which was more like a familiar scar than an open wound now.

She felt sure, now, that she had shut up the man of her childhood dreams in a corner of her mind which had always been reserved for him. Serenely, she let herself indulge in memories which she thought could no longer hurt.

She imagined a figure in a white dinner jacket, slowly waltzing over the pale oak floor. One by one, in her mind's eye, she switched on the chandeliers. As if in a magic spell, men and women came out on the floor – delicate, clear-eyed dolls in lace, grey lead soldiers. The music grew louder, and the couples linked arms to the sound of rustling taffeta. The murmur of other guests' voices was a rhythmical accompaniment to the music, punctuated by the clink of crystal glasses.

Sandra looked for the man in the white dinner jacket. He seemed to have disappeared. Peals of laughter rang out under the moulding, where coquettish cherubs chased each other, never catching up. The girls were already taking their partners away for an hour or a night of love. Sitting on the piano stool, Sandra pursued her imaginary vision.

The waltz was running away with itself – like her dream. Sighs of ecstasy rose from the depths of the sofas. A girl had begun to sing. Her voice seemed to caress the dancers, who moved on the pale wood floor, swaying voluptuously. Someone had opened a window, and the noise of the party spread out into the courtyard, travelled all round the house and came back, like an echo, to die on the piano notes.

Sandra suddenly saw him close to the fireplace, his face hidden by a black mask.

One foot crossed casually over the other, left elbow resting in his right hand, he was holding something, she could not quite see what. An ironical smile on his lips, he came slowly towards her. Suddenly he was behind her, and a hand was placed on her shoulder – a perfectly real hand, whose touch she knew.

'Good evening, Sandra.'

She closed her eyes. Her fingers were motionless on the white keys. The drawing room was dark and silent again, and the man placed a kiss which drew a shiver from her in the hollow of her throat.

'Marc, I've . . .'

Tenderly, he placed a hand over her mouth.

'Don't let's talk just now.'

He stripped the silk kimono from Sandra's shoulders, drawing its sleeves off her arms, and the silken fabric fell softly round her waist. She let herself lie back against him. Still standing behind her, he cupped her breasts in his hands.

'Tomorrow other men will see you and want you – and some of them, a chosen few, will have you! This evening, I want you all to myself, as if it were the very first time.'

He raised her from the piano stool and turned her round, to embrace her.

Pressed to Marc's body, Sandra leaned back against the piano. His mouth passed over her breasts. Slowly, he undid the belt of the kimono, uncovering her pearly nakedness.

He sat on the piano stool, his mouth level with Sandra's mount of Venus. Roused by the sight of her white buttocks on the black and white piano keys, he stroked her bush of auburn hair with both hands, delicately parting her red vaginal lips to drink her juices.

Head thrown back, Sandra moaned. Her hips rose and fell rhythmically, meeting the tongue exploring inside her.

Abruptly, Marc stopped. A little groan of frustration escaped Sandra. With both hands, she tried to draw his head back again.

But Marc had straightened up. Taking out his penis, he penetrated Sandra with one thrust of his loins. She bit her lip, but could not help crying out. She felt the rough texture of Marc's suit against her bare skin. Her nipples were erect, brown on white.

The penis thrusting inside her was so familiar, yet she felt she was discovering it for the first time. There was a bitter-sweet flavour in her mouth. Sandra told herself she could never tire of that hard shaft of flesh, or the way Marc made love.

She was almost sitting on the piano, clinging to Marc's shoulders as if to imprint her skin on him, leaving her mark there.

How I love his body, she thought, before flowing away into a liquid world. An instinct deep inside her told her she could not do without this man – the man who had bent her to his will, who both fascinated and repelled her, who had hurt her and would not hesitate to do so again.

She came to her climax, the orgasm overtaking her like a

slow wave rising and breaking over her taut body. They both slid to the floor and lay there for a long time, still caressing each other.

Sandra opened her eyes. The greyness of the sky showed her dawn was near. Looking round, she saw the furnishing of the room resume their ordinary shape. That was what she wanted just now. The whole house seemed to be wrapped in a silky cocoon. She felt she was on solid ground, for the first time in her life.

'You know, Marc,' she murmured into the hollow of his shoulder, 'I'd never have believed it, but I can't wait to begin.'

She licked her lips. He was awake too, as she could tell from the beating of his heart against her skin.

'I believe I'm going to enjoy it,' she added.

'Because you'll be able to put your talents to the test – am I right?' he said, sitting up.

He took possession of her mouth, kissing her with surprising violence.

'I shall have to get used to seeing you even less often,' he went on calmly.

'Yes.' She smiled, affectionately. 'I'm glad you're keeping the apartment in the Avenue Théophile-Gautier on. You'll need somewhere to sleep while I'm . . . working.'

'Little imp!'

He rolled her back on the carpet and stroked her breasts again, but this time she pushed him away.

'Let's go and finish the night in my room, Marc. I'd like to start with a transformation scene. After all – this is my last night as a respectable married woman and a diplomat's wife, isn't it?'

They both rose. Leaving their clothes in the drawing room, they climbed the stairs to Sandra's room together.

Marc opened the door and stood back to let her go first, bowing her in with formal correctitude.

'Good evening, Madame l'Ambassadrice!' he murmured, half tender and half ironic.

Head held high, she preceded him into the room. She did not much mind what Marc was thinking. She felt a shiver run down her spine.

That very evening she would be ringing up the curtain.

III

JAMES

11

The big red drawing room looked festive. Champagne made the girls' eyes sparkle. They were hovering like so many colourful dragonflies around the men who had come – though they did not know it – to celebrate the Unicorn's second anniversary.

Sandra, dressed in emerald green, moved serenely among the guests. She stopped one of the waitresses carrying laden trays and took a glass, before gliding over to the piano, where she whispered a word or so in the ear of the tall black pianist. He went into a langourous blues.

During these two years, life at the Unicorn had seemed like one long celebration. A celebration of the body and the senses. Sandra made very sure that all the clients left the establishment remembering it as an oasis of delicious pleasure, of exquisite indulgence in lust and sensual delights. They often came back. By now, the address of the very exclusive brothel was known to diplomats and businessmen from all over the world. She knew from Marc that ministers often sent their distinguished guests to her when they expressed a wish for a good time. Sandra had remembered the lessons she learned from Ice during her forced apprenticeship in Casablanca. Madame l'Ambassadrice, as Laure sometimes called her, gently teasing, "Madam Ambassadress", had become mistress of ceremonies for the more daring pleasures of the great men of the world.

Her first triumph, shortly after the place opened, was the occasion when a plump little man in tortoiseshell-rimmed glasses presented himself at the door. Behind him, at the top of the steps, stood a so-called secretary with a bodyguard's physique. The little man with the wavy fair hair, who was so careful about his cover name, pretended to have got the wrong address at first. (Not so the secretary-cum-bodyguard, who without more ado made straight for Fedora the Argentinian girl.) He had blinked his myopic eyes as he looked the girls over, smiled broadly, and then, in nasal American, ordered champagne as if he were merely bowing with a good grace to the accident which had led him to this hospitable but decidedly improper place. Hands crossed over his plump stomach, he launched into a fascinating account of termites and their way of life – until he caught sight of Maya entering the room with the majestic grace of an Ethiopian princess. Captivated, he immediately put down his glass, drew himself up to his full height, which was not much, and kissed the hand she held out before taking it in his.

As he followed the Ethiopian girl to her room, relishing the sight of her swaying hips, Laure hurried over to Sandra.

'Did you recognize him? That's the famous American economist who – '

Sandra silenced her with a loud kiss on the lips. It was the rule at the Unicorn never to utter the real names of their famous clients. Even the heir to one of the most prestigious thrones of Europe went under an alias here.

Sometimes Marc himself played host to an Arab prince or some such dignitary at the Unicorn. Sandra asked her husband no questions. The affairs of ministers of state were none of her business. She was satisfied with knowing that an important agreement might depend upon a visit here. A man with his senses gratified and his body relaxed is more likely to make concessions, even financial ones.

Leafing through a magazine, she had once recognized the dictator of a South American state as the man who visited the Unicorn every time he was passing through Paris, to be whipped by Kazuko with handfuls of freshly cut nettles. He brought them himself, carrying them like a bouquet.

Almost every state visit filled Sandra's drawing rooms. The girls' orders were to satisfy the most intimate desires of the visiting dignitaries, while letting them talk freely. Many state secrets were confided to the softness of a breast or the curve of a hip.

Standing by the fireplace, Laure was surveying the results of their long months of work. Sandra joined her there.

'Many happy returns!' murmured Laure, raising her glass to Sandra.

'To both of us!' Sandra replied. 'To all of us!'

Without needing to say so, each knew the other was thinking back over the past. A dreamy look in her eyes, Laure patted Sandra's shoulder.

'You remember that African king . . . ?

Sandra momentarily pressed close to her friend in response to the caress, and then immediately moved away. Madame l'Ambassadrice did not show her feelings in public.

'He came here after a reception at the Opera,' Laure went on, 'and ordered sausage and red wine! And then . . . '

Sandra smiled, and took up the story.

'And then he wanted the two of us to play with each other in front of him, while the other girls made love to his bodyguard, sitting astride them!'

Laure emptied her glass. 'Oh, what an orgasm I had that night – with you! It would have lasted longer if he hadn't been so excited he wanted me almost at once. My God, was he brutal!'

'But generous,' Sandra pointed out. 'Yes, indeed! He gave me diamonds by way of an apology,' Laure laughed. 'A whole handful of diamonds which he happened to have in his pocket. I had them made into pendants and a necklace. Look . I'm wearing some of them this evening. You're not still envious, are you? *You've* got nothing to complain of! There's that Deputy who brings you a rose once a month, before asking for Shanah!'

They both burst out laughing. Laure threw her head back, letting the light of the chandeliers sparkle on her diamonds.

'Why isn't Marc here?' she asked.

Sandra's smile was a little forced. She sipped champagne.

'Would you take a glass of wine up to the technician, Laure? And take the opportunity of seeing everything's all right upstairs.'

'Fine – I'll go up.'

She put her glass down on the mantelpiece, hesitated, and then repeated her question. '*Isn't* he coming this evening?'

'Who?'

'Marc, of course.'

'I don't think so.'

Laure gave a little shrug of her shoulders before going off into the hall.

Sandra turned her attention to the men in the drawing room. That young secretary from the American Embassy had chosen Jill again, she saw, noticing one couple make for the big staircase leading up to the bedrooms. He must be one of those Americans who thought nothing was any good unless it came from the States, whisky and women included! and Jill was the Romanian military adviser's favourite, too.

She checked the smile rising to her lips and looked at the sofa in the middle of the room, where a delegate from the Arab League, a new client, was hesitating between Ingrid and Bettina. Both blondes, of course. If he only knew that an Israeli envoy had been sitting in that exact spot just a month earlier! Despite two years' experience, Sandra was still surprised to find how easy it was to predict a man's sexual preferences. Since the place opened she had seen all sorts of men pass through her doors. Some she admired, others she despised. She had given herself to many of them – and not one of them had managed to surprise her.

Well, yes – perhaps she *had* been surprised once! By a high-up Saudi functionary and a Mexican delegate on a trade mission. They had happened to meet in the drawing room, by chance, and went up to Maria's room together.

But without Maria. When Sandra, rather intrigued, went into the control room to see what was up, she saw them both sitting on Maria's bed in their short-sleeves, in front of a pocket calculator, talking petrodollars.

She had not been entirely reassured until they came back next day, separately. Each of them visited the room again, this time *with* Maria, who never knew that a rise in the price of a barrel of oil had been negotiated there on her bed.

Two more couples left the room. In an hour's time the five trade delegates would arrive. They had made a group booking for all the girls, politely requesting the presence of Madame l'Ambassadrice as well, to celebrate their appointment. This one was worth following up. There would certainly be useful information to be gleaned. When men came in a party they were talkative. They seemed to feel the need to intoxicate themselves with words, and prided themselves on the names and figures they could quote to the girls at their feet. Especially military men. Often, senior NATO officers came to the Unicorn after going on manouevres, to enjoy a warrior's repose. Their military correctness came off with their uniforms, and they boasted of their exploits as if they were all field marshals describing their campaigns – while the girls encouraged them to talk as they pampered their tired bodies.

She told herself that she ought to try and see Marc tonight. Perhaps he had looked in at the Avenue Théophile-Gautier, or he might have left a message. But somehow, she didn't feel like it.

Laure had just appeared in the doorway of the drawing room. She made a little gesture which told Sandra that all was well.

'I'm going up to my office for a moment,' said Sandra. 'Let me know when the girls come down again.'

Slowly, she climbed to the second floor and opened the door of her little coral-coloured world. She took a Benson and Hedges cigarette from a little gilt box on the desk. Ice, that red spider of a woman, used to smoke the same brand in the Café Américain in Casablanca. The memory brought a fleeting smile to Sandra's face. She automatically tapped the gilded box with one lacquered nail. Sandra treasured that box and thought more of it than Laure's diamonds, though it was worth less in itself. It was one of those souvenirs that are more precious than jewels . . .

The man had been tall and well built. His eyes remained cold in spite of his smile. Before slowly undressing him as he lay on the bed, Sandra had dropped a kiss on the cleft in the determined chin, grazing her lips on the stubble of his beard. She unbuttoned his white shirt and then stroked his chest, tangling her fingers in the grey hairs on his torso. He uttered a moan of pleasure – the first sound she had heard from him since he arrived. He had not even replied to her words of welcome fifteen minutes earlier. Was he discourteous or just shy?

A distinguished civil servant who was a friend of Marc's had arrived the night before to give her notice of this man's visit. Sandra had had the camera in Room 6 disconnected. This was the room that a visitor could reach by way of an emergency entrance at the back of the building, with no need to pass through the drawing rooms or up the main staircase. She asked Laure to take over for her at the door and in the drawing rooms: this was her usual practice whenever she went into action herself. Because she wanted to attend to this mysterious visitor personally. She knew all about his reputation for toughness; his quick temper and changes of mood were frequently mentioned in the papers. Apparently, adventure amused and excited him.

He seemed ill as ease and suspicious. Yet it was all just as he had specified. The bed was made up with lavender-scented black satin sheets. A pink light shed a rosy glow over the comfort of the room. Underneath her kimono, Sandra was wearing black net stockings and a black suspender belt, which set off the pearly whiteness of her thighs and the auburn of her pubic hair. He helped her slide his trousers down his sturdy legs himself. He was a little thick about the hips – that would be his age, but even more so the lack of physical exercise.

A handsome man, all the same. His penis surprised Sandra. It was thick and long. But despite her preliminary caresses it lay limp. His eyes were still closed, his smile was supercilious. Sandra was going to need all her erotic skill to transform that enormous icicle into a brazier.

She guessed that she must not hurry this enigmatic visitor of hers. She knelt beside his lower abdomen and began licking him, nibbling gently at the skin around his navel. She felt him begin to stir and move under the light and stimulating touch of her mouth. Slowly, it passed over his hip and thigh, avoiding the still flaccid penis, and down to his ankles. Sliding her head between the sheet and his legs, she dropped several light kisses behind his knees. He moved in surprise. She went farther down to suck his heels, one by one. His penis was swelling. Now she could begin on the second part of the foreplay.

Lying on top of him, she gently kissed his shoulders and breathed warm kisses into the hollows of his ears, licking their lobes. She felt his penis hardening against her thighs. His supercilious smile had gone. She looked deep into his eyes, and it was like a signal. He raised his arms and tugged at the neck of her kimono to free her breasts, which he cupped in his hands with a sigh of pleasure. She gently withdrew, straightening up so that he could see her in all her provocative near-nakedness. The rosy lamplight cast a watered-silk effect on her legs, smooth in their stockings. Her kimono slipped to the floor. He put out his hand to the burning bush of her pubic hair, insinuating a forefinger into the sweet groove between her thighs.

All these preliminaries had aroused Sandra too, and once it reached the lubricated slit the man's finger had no trouble finding its way in. His caresses became firmer. She let a moan escape her. Intrigued, the man looked at her, and went on with what he was doing. Sandra's pleasure was not faked. The dripping wetness of his hand told him what an effect he was having on her. With a heave of his loins, he turned her over on the black satin sheet and leaned over her body. Its flesh seemed to gleam white in contrast with the sheet.

Sandra took his face between her hands, cupped as if in prayer, and drew it downwards to her. 'Lick me! Lick me – deep down there!'

With a hoarse gasp of desire he obeyed, avoiding her guiding hands and making his own way towards the palpitating wide-spread slit she offered him, while she seized his huge erection, massaging him in time to the rhythm of his tongue setting her own genitals on fire.

Suddenly he straightened up. He was a great, grey-maned stallion. Sandra could not remember ever having seen such a long, thick penis. Moaning, she cried out to him, all the suppleness of her hips welcoming him into her. His battering ram stretched her, hurting deliciously deep inside. She bit her lips so as not to cry out with her pleasure. Her strange partner seemed almost amused by her ecstasies, her violent desire, the tossing of her head framed in its red ringlets on the sheet.

Slowly, he pulled out of her, a gleam of laughter in the depths of his crinkled eyes. She felt that smooth withdrawal as a wrench, a loss. She wanted it back, she begged for it, eyes frenzied with desire. Her mute pleading both amused the world-weary man and seemed to fan his pleasure. He kneaded her buttocks, holding the end of his huge penis across her vaginal lips, just beyond the reach of her avid vulva.

In a sudden moment of lucidity Sandra saw how he was dominating her. Well, she would have her revenge! An old Oriental trick! With a sudden movement, she freed herself from the man's embrace.

Taken aback, he watched her search the drawer of a dressing table, similar to those in all the rooms at the Unicorn and standing beside the bathroom door. She produced a necklace of large imitation pearls and a tube of lubricating jelly.

'You surprised me,' she said, 'and now it's my turn to surprise you!'

She made him lie on his stomach. He seemed intrigued, but he had not got that annoying smile back. With a certain perverse amusement, she pulled her net stockings up on her thighs and re-adjusted her suspenders before leaning over the big body that awaited her caresses.

Her fingers, lubricated with the jelly, made their way down the groove between her partner's buttocks and penetrated the anus. Then she slowly pushed the pearl necklace as far in as she could. He quivered at first and then gave himself up to this new sensation.

'Now – come back inside me!'

Sandra slipped underneath him, holding up her mouth for a passionate kiss. They were both burning with desire, their skins close, the pent-up violence uniting their bodies. Sandra clasped the greying head into the hollow of her shoulder with one hand while she held the end of the necklace with the other.

As they made powerful, majestic love she pulled out the pearls one by one, keeping in time with the rise and fall of their bodies. Once she guessed, from feeling the spasms that shook him, he was about to come, she pulled out the rest of the necklace all at once at the critical moment, giving him an extraordinarily intense orgasm. He uttered a deep, gutteral cry of pleasure while his semen flooded over Sandra's own dilated flesh.

They lay locked together for a long time, greedily breathing in the sweet, sharp odours rising from their satisfied bodies.

'Thank you,' he said. 'Thank you for the pleasure you have given me.'

Those were the only words he had spoken throughout – in careful French with a heavy accent.

Next day, an officer in an ornate uniform got out of a Diplomatic Corps car with a small parcel for Sandra. It contained a large pearl, inside the gilded box. A Gothic letter S was engraved on the luminous pearl in fine gold.

'A gift from our President,' stated the officer, before clicking his heels and turning to leave, his sword under his arm.

Sandra flipped over the pages of her appointments diary, and made a face. She'd forgotten about that tea party with the Romanian vice-consul's wife, to which she and Marc were invited the next day. It suddenly struck her that Marc had been very keen on forming closer ties with the countries of the Eastern bloc recently. Only two days earlier they had been to a reception at the Polish Embassy, and she seemed to remember that they were soon to attend a Bolshoi Ballet première, followed by a supper party at the Soviet Embassy.

Without much real curiosity, she wondered whether Marc was engaged in some undercover operation she didn't know about, when the telephone went, shrill and monotonous. She let it ring three times and then lifted the receiver.

'Yes?'

'Sandra, there's something wrong in Room 8,' said the technician. 'You'd better come and look.'

His voice was tense and worried. Sandra went a little pale and hung up without a word. Toni, the lovely Dutch girl, was in Room 8 with Colonel Anderson, a NATO official who had become a regular visitor to the Unicorn over the last few weeks. His sessions with the girl had been studied with great interest. He seemed to be remarkably talkative when amorous, and Toni was one of the Unicorn's best recruits. The colonel had seemed to be on very good form during his recent visits; it would be remarkably bad luck to have him go the same way as that cardinal who died of a heart attack in Ingrid's arms. Marc, who had been informed at once, had the body taken to an apartment on the other side of Paris. The press had accepted the police version of events, and no newspaper stories had mentioned the Unicorn.

Sandra hurried to a little door hidden by a curtain and entered the control room.

This was a small, windowless room, with no decoration and hardly any furniture. There were just two chairs in front of a large grey metal console, sober and impressive as the deck of an aircraft carrier. One wall was covered with screens: twelve colour television sets which were, so to speak, the Unicorn's eyes and ears. There were also four video recorders running the whole time under the impassive eye of a young, shirt-sleeved technician, who was always absolutely discreet and courteous. The technicians worked in six-hour shifts, relieving each other, but it always seemed to Sandra to be the same man, impersonal and taciturn.

She was proud of this "laboratory", where love-play was transformed into valuable information. She was proud of her team of lovely Mata Haris too. Even men professionally trained to keep silent would let themselves be drawn into confidences in the arms of her girls. Those confidences were immediately recorded, and went to be sorted, dissected and analysed by the French intelligence services. Marc saw to this undercover dealing in video cassettes and reels of film outside the Unicorn. He would warn Sandra when a client had a reputation for being a tough nut to crack, and in such cases Sandra did not hesitate to give herself, generously. She rarely failed. Madame l'Ambassadrice knew how to unlock tongues.

She knew Marc had watched her at work several times, in the control room. As if he needed to be a voyeur to become a better lover.

'Yes?' she asked.

'Here,' said the young technician. 'Look.'

He pointed to a screen in the top row.

Sandra looked at the picture it showed. Naked from the waist up, Colonel Anderson was holding the blonde girl's arm. He seemed furious, and was shaking her roughly.

'Turn the sound up, Michel,' said Sandra briskly.

'You little tart!' the colonel was shouting. 'You think I

didn't see you search my attaché case?'

'But . . . but . . . ' Toni stammered.

The man slapped her hard.

'I'm going in there,' said Sandra. 'Tell Laure at once, will you? Ask her to come up here too.'

She left the control room by the door leading to the landing and ran down to the first floor, driven by a single thought: she *must* prevent any scandal. Silently, she cursed Marc for not being there.

She met Laure outside Room 8.

'What's going on?'

'It's Toni's client – not satisfied with the service, apparently,' explained Sandra, producing the master key she always carried.

Though all the rooms were soundproofed, they could hear the colonel's shouts from out on the landing.

'You look after Toni,' said Sandra. 'I'll deal with the colonel.'

She swiftly turned the key in the lock and went in, closing the door after her.

The man immediately turned to her. Toni was weeping on the bed, her head in her hands.

'Good evening, Colonel,' said Sandra calmly. 'Can I help you?' She wore a practised smile on her face.

'I certainly hope so! It's about time I saw you, madame!' began the man. He had an American accent, and his reddish-blond moustache was quivering with indignation as he went on. 'Look here, I had this place of yours recommended to me as the very best in Paris, and – '

'And that is exactly what it is!' interrupted Sandra. 'If you would be good enough to tell me your problem, Colonel . . . ?'

'It's this little whore here,' he began, pointing to Toni. 'I was getting undressed, and she took advantage of that to search my briefcase!'

'Colonel, there must be some mistake. All our staff are hand-picked – and this is not the first time you've availed yourself to Toni's services.'

'No, but I can damn well assure you it's going to be the last!'

And before Sandra could make any move at all, the colonel had taken Toni's arm and forced her to get to her feet. He dragged her over to the door, which he flung open. Then he pushed the girl out of the room.

'That's how I deal with her sort,' he thundered.

Laure, waiting on the landing, took Toni in her arms. At this moment a man came out of the next room, adjusting his tie, and looked curiously at the scene.

The colonel addressed him. 'Better keep an eye on your things, my dear fellow! This place is a bloody nest of vipers!'

His voice echoed in the stairwell, and must be audible in the drawing rooms on the ground floor. Several clients, hearing the noise, had come out into the hall and were looking up.

Sandra went over to the colonel, took his arm and firmly guided him back into the room.

'My dear Colonel, we must have a little talk,' she purred, without relaxing her grip.

Simultaneously, she signalled imperiously to Laure, who handed Toni over to the girl emerging from the other room, slid her arm into that of the client whom the colonel addressed, and walked downstairs with him, making amusing light conversation about the effects alcohol had on some people.

Sandra closed the door after her. The trickiest part was over. Now she had to pacify Anderson. She knew very well the man was lying. Toni would never have made such a stupid blunder. So what did he want? Scandal for scandal's sake.

She looked at the colonel's flushed face, observing his fair hair, which was wavy and tinged with grey at the temples, while his beard and moustache were almost red. His intense blue eyes might have been artificial, and he had a long scar on his right cheek. From the War? Was he old enough to have fought in it? Well, the point was that he was far from pacified just now! He was marching round the room, swearing profusely, and twirling the ends of his moustache. Sandra went over to him and put a hand on his naked shoulder.

'Colonel, do sit down. I owe you an apology.'

He stopped his maddening pacing, and turned to face her.

'Oh yes? And just what do you expect me to do with an apology?' he shot at her.

Involuntarily, Sandra withdrew her hand. Then, pulling herself together, she said, 'Colonel, it was only an isolated incident. I shall take good care such a thing never happens to you again.'

'Always supposing I ever visit this place again!' he growled.

'Well, I think you might well want to when you've seen what my apology is like,' she replied coaxingly, gently urging him down on the bed. Her hands ran over his torso, caressing and soothing him. 'Just relax,' she murmured into his ear.

She put out the bedside lamp and switched on a tiny nightlight which diffused a pink, almost unreal glow. Her mouth slid over the man's neck, brushing past his shoulders. Her tongue licked over his torso, making its way down towards his flat stomach. She felt his rigid body gradually relax. When she undid the belt of his trousers he lay down for a moment to let her take them off.

Sandra finished undressing him. She was slightly surprised to find that he already had an erection. She took his penis in her hands and caressed it, then placed her lips around its warm shaft. The colonel was lying there in an attitude of abandon as surprising as the brutality of his behaviour earlier on. Sandra's mouth toyed with his penis, drawing a moan of pleasure from him. His haunches moved gently as she caressed him.

Whenever she chose to see to a client's needs personally, Sandra closed her mind to everything outside the room, and she did so now. She forgot she was Madame l'Ambassadrice. She would think of nothing but pleasure . . . and she realized that it did give her great pleasure to take this penis in her mouth. She liked its texture, its suppleness, its warmth, the way it responded to her attentions.

Totally absorbed in the sensation of having that penis throbbing at the back of her mouth, Sandra did not notice that the Colonel had raised himself slightly and was looking at her. Suddenly he grasped her shoulders, freed himself, and drew her close.

'What . . . ' Sandra began, surprised once more by the man's sudden move.

'I want to make love to you,' he whispered, and he slid on top of her, covering her with his body.

His fingers moved over the fabric of her dress, crumpling it, seeking for the silkily rough texture of her auburn fleece of hair. She made it easy for him, stretching her thighs and parting her knees. With a grunt of satisfaction, he made his way into the vagina lying open to him, pushing himself slowly and with all his might up inside her.

Once again, Sandra noticed something that always surprised her: the moment when the man with her ceased to be a stranger. Then everything happened very fast and she lost track of time. Giving another groan of satisfaction, Anderson began to thrust. There was something in his love-making that was both violent and tender, filling her up and leaving her still open to him, so that Sandra somehow felt she was not in a room with a difficult client any more, but hovering in some other place where only sensation counted.

Her hips rose to meet the man's. She clung to his muscular back, cried out uncontrollably, sought for his mouth as she surrendered herself to his hard penis.

'Sandra!' said the man, as he felt her rising to orgasm.

And in the stranger's arms, Madame l'Ambassadrice came and came.

She was dressed again, and the colonel, lying on the bed, was smoking a cigarette.

'I must go now,' said Sandra. 'And since you accepted my apology,' she added with a mischievous smile, 'I hope to see you in my establishment again soon! Good evening, Colonel.'

He did not speak or move. Sandra left the room and went upstairs to her own quarters again. She took a quick shower and then rang Laure.

A few moments later the blonde girl opened the door of her room.

'Did everything go all right downstairs?'

'No problems there,' said Laure. 'They put it down to too much champagne.'

'How's Toni?'

'She's okay. I told her to go and get some sleep.'

Obviously the tale of the briefcase had not the least foundation in fact. One might have thought the man deliberately wanted to make trouble and rouse the whole place.

'A strange man,' said Sandra slowly. 'I don't quite see what he was after. I must tell Marc about it, and we'll have to keep an eye on him. Anyway, I think I managed to calm him down.'

Laure laughed. 'I met him going downstairs as I was coming up. He was on his way out, and he looked quiet as a lamb.'

'Good. Well, I suppose that party of five has arrived.'

'They're waiting patiently in the white drawing room.'

Sandra tossed back her hair. 'Well, come on, Laure, we've a long night ahead of us.'

It was four in the morning when Sandra went up to her private rooms again.

In the solitude of her bedroom, she undressed and slipped between clean sheets, her body weary and her mind troubled. Marc won't be coming tonight, she thought. The evening's events were still going round and round in her head. Colonel Anderson intrigued her more than she would have thought possible; she just could not understand why he had behaved as he did. Could he have realized that he had been under surveillance when he came to the house. What kind of trouble was he trying to make? And why had she let herself go so unrestrainedly with him?

Sleep suddenly overcame her, as if in mocking reply to her questions.

A slight sound woke her. Her hand went out to the little digital alarm clock on her bedside table. Its luminous face showed that the time was five-thirty. Sandra swung her feet out of bed, tossed back the abundant hair that half covered her face, and went to find the source of the sound.

It was coming from the control room! From where she stood, all she could see was the curtain drawn over the doorway. She must have forgotten to close the door itself. No light came through the thick fabric, but Sandra was sure someone was playing back a video cassette in there.

Barefoot, she went silently to the doorway, her heels sinking into the carpet. It won't be Laure, she thought. Nor one of the girls. A technician, perhaps. Or . . .

She was close to the curtain now. Yes, the door had been left open, and now she could see a faint light: probably from a torch. Her heart began to beat faster.

She moved a little to the left, to get a better view of the interior of the control room. A man was seated at the console. The torch lit up his fair hair and the hard lines of his face from below. His hands were running over the controls, pressing a switch here, lowering a slider there. His gaze was riveted to the screen, where Sandra saw herself in Colonel Anderson's arms.

She froze. Why was Marc playing back this cassette, unknown to her? She had hoped to have time to destroy it tomorrow before the arrival of the day technician. Then she saw that another video recorder was running. Marc was copying the cassette. Why? Who for? A kind of daze prevented her from thinking. She watched, standing in her dark corner and listening to her husband's hoarse breathing. She was disturbed. Deeply disturbed. Then, on the screen, the American moved away from her. She could see herself there, vulva exposed and gleaming with his semon and her own juices, the proof of her orgasm. At last the picture flickered and disappeared.

Marc took the cassette he had just copied out of the recorder and then pressed a key down. Another screen lit up, and the interplay of the two bodies began again.

For his own pleasure this time, thought Sandra bitterly. What's he going to do with the copy? She preferred not to try working out the answer to that question just now. She began planning what she would say in a moment's time when she turned on the lights in the control room.

The telephone went.

Sandra started, and hurried back to her bedroom, blessing the thick carpet which muffled her footsteps. Her hand was shaking slightly as she lifted the receiver. Over in the control room, there was a dry little click, followed by the sound of a door closing.

'Yes?' Sandra said softly.

'Alexandra? Sandra? Is that you?'

The voice quavered a little, as if worn by years of servitude.

Sandra hardly hesitated. 'Adèle! It's been so long! What is it?'

A flood of memories submerged her, and for a few seconds she could hardly speak. The old governess broke the silence, giving her news in a rush.

'Oh, Alexandra – your father's very ill. He's just had a heart attack, and he wants to see you. Can you come at once?'

Adrien's face, his rather dry, intimidating manner of speaking . . .

'Now? Oh, Adèle . . . ' She stopped, said nothing for a moment or so, and then replied in a firm voice. 'Yes. I'll be there in an hour's time.'

12

Versailles had just been signposted off on the right. Sandra sat back in the grey leather seat and stretched her stiff arms without letting go of the wheel. A sigh escaped her pale lips. Her thoughts, which had hitherto been concentrating on the tangle of intersections, had free play now she was on the straight line of the autoroute.

In her mind's eye, she once again saw Laure's surprise when she woke her friend to say where she was going.

'Your father? I didn't even know you had one!'

'I hardly knew myself, Laure. I'd almost forgotten him.'

'Surely you're not setting off on your own at this time of night?'

'Go back to sleep – I just wanted to tell you. I really *don't* need a nursemaid, you know!'

'I'm not so sure,' Laure had muttered, yawning.

Sandra kept the secret of Marc's nocturnal visit to herself. She felt she had stumbled on something important here, and instinct told her to keep quiet. Marc had broken a pact they made when the Unicorn opened: a tacit agreement that she herself would never be seen with a client on the videotapes stored in the control room. She had always had the right to destroy any cassettes showing herself as and when she pleased. Now, Sandra realized only too well that she had been deceived. Marc might have copies of all the cassettes made during these two years, including those which she had thought were destroyed. There was nothing to prove that the scene in the control room had not taken place a hundred times before, in the privacy of a grey dawn. And Sandra guessed there was something more at stake here than a simple matter of voyeurism.

Her glance automatically went to a sign on her right.

Rambouillet 20 kilometres. The name brought a taste of mulberries into her mouth. She wanted to forget about Marc and his intrigues; she tried to remember how long it was since she had last seen her father. It took a serious illness to make him want to see her again! Sandra turned this thought over in her mind for several minutes, like a child touching a graze to see if it still hurts.

Yes, it *was* a sensitive place, but the pain seemed bearable. Sandra realized that the last five years of her life had widened the gulf between her father and herself, but oddly enough, the idea did not disturb her. She had grown away from the dreams of her own family – or was it that the life she led had armoured her to the point where she was almost invulnerable?

The first lights of Rambouillet twinkled through her windscreen. As surely as she had once ridden the stable lad's Solex, she now drove the BMW through the winding streets of the town she thought she had forgotten. The Rue des Alouettes brought her to the old house with its dark façade. Only the alleyway leading to the garage was lit up. Sandra slowed down and let the car glide up to the open garage door.

The garage was empty. She put the BMW away, wondering if her father's illness had forced him to give up driving. Switching off the ignition, she got out of the car. To her left, behind the heavy wooden door, she saw the remains of a Solex. Rusty, covered with dust, resting on its stand. It had no wheels or handlebars left, and the back mudguard was twisted.

Sandra opened the gate leading into the garden. Her footsteps crunched on the gravel. Her senses picked up a confused medley of scents and flavours. In the dark, her childhood home suddenly seemed a disturbing place. The ivy which covered it had grown, masking some of the windows, twining round the shutters, hanging an overheavy cloak of foliage on the walls.

The garden had been neglected. Brambles had replaced

the lupins and irises. Sandra shivered and hurried towards the steps up to the house. She saw a small, dark, dumpy figure standing on them. Adèle always had good hearing, she thought, climbing the first step. The whinny of a horse startled her. Hers, perhaps? Did he remember her, and the sugar lumps she used to give him after a ride? If he was still alive . . .

'Good evening, Sandra.'

'Hullo, Adèle.' She leaned towards her old governess and embraced her affectionately.

Adèle stifled a sob and hurried back into the house, taking Sandra with her.

'How is he?'

'Dr Blanchot's here,' said Adèle, sniffling. 'And there's a cardiologist, and a nurse, and all those machines . . . '

The rest was lost in the white handkerchief the governess was holding in front of her face. Sandra put an arm round her shoulders.

'There, there – let's go and see him, Adèle.'

'I . . . I don't know if you'll be able to see him straight away. They're in the middle of doing something – and there are tubes everywhere.'

'Let's go up, all the same,' said Sandra.

The two women climbed the big dark wooden staircase. There was still a smell of beeswax that Sandra disliked about the place.

'Wait a moment, Sandra. I'll see if you can go in.'

'But . . .'

Adèle had disappeared inside the room before Sandra could finish what she was saying, and she came out again a few moments later.

'You must wait. They say you can't see him just now.'

'What do you mean, *they?*' cried Sandra, suddenly losing her temper. 'I'd like to know who's going to keep me from seeing Adrien!'

She put her hand on the door knob and began to turn it. The door gave way.

'I am, mademoiselle! And I really must ask you to make less noise.'

The nurse came on to the landing and closed the door behind her. She had the stern look of a mature woman used to commanding an army of young girls. A grave, dry voice, a grey-skinned face as if she took off her make-up with formaldehyde. Despite herself, Sandra stepped back.

'In any case, mademoiselle, who are you?' asked the nurse.

Adèle stammered something. Sandra felt her jaws tense with rage.

'I am Alexandra de Moncet!' she snapped. 'And the man you are guarding so jealously is my father. Now, if you will be kind enough to let me pass . . . '

Sandra walked round the nurse and took hold of the doorknob again.

'Oh – Mademoiselle de Moncet! One moment, please.' Her tone was softer, but the voice was still authoritarian. 'I'm afraid you can't go in just now. Professor Michaux is busy examining your father, who is in a very serious condition. I am very sorry, but you'll have to wait.'

Sandra was about to make a cutting reply when Adèle intervened.

'Come along, Sandra, I'll make you some tea.' And turning to the nurse, she said, 'Thank you, mademoiselle. We'll wait.'

The governess took Sandra's arm and led her along the landing, and the nurse went back into the room.

'Please calm down, Sandra,' said Adèle.

'Let me go!'

Sandra shook herself free, but Adèle was looking at her so sadly that her anger subsided.

'I'm sorry, Adèle. I didn't mean to hurt you.' She planted a kiss on the wrinkled cheek. 'My nerves are all on edge, that's the trouble. You make that tea if you like, and I'll be with you in five minutes' time. Jasmine tea – you always used to make jasmine tea.'

Adèle nodded slowly and went downstairs, carefully holding the rail.

Left alone, Sandra went to the double casement window which looked out on the gardens behind the house. She rested her forehead against the cold glass, looking out into the dark. A small light on the terrace was on. Beyond it, the approaching dawn showed the tops of the poplar trees. Sandra felt deserted and forgotten.

She left the window. Her footsteps led her to her old bedroom, in search of the peaceful past. She opened the door and went in. Nothing here had changed. The quilted bedspread, the satin cushions, her books on the shelves – all her old familiar world seemed to be waiting for her. She went over to the bed, bent down and picked up a tattered old Ian Fleming book from the floor on the right of her pillow. She caressed it for a moment before putting it on the shelf with the others. Her James Bond collection! *The Spy Who Loved Me*. It's like a museum, she thought. A museum of my past. She uttered a brief, bitter little laugh.

When Sandra came out of the room Adèle was waiting for her on the landing.

'I've been looking for you everywhere – I thought you'd left! Tea's ready in the drawing room.'

Sandra said nothing. She followed the governess to the big, over-furnished room. Half the armchairs were covered with dust sheets now, and so were the two sofas, but the little coffee table was uncovered. Adèle placed a cup and a steaming teapot on it.

'Aren't you having any tea?' asked Sandra.

'No, my dear, it's for you.'

Standing up, Sandra drank a mouthful of the hot liquid. She noticed that there were new curtains, and their colour no longer matched the rest of the drawing room.

'Sit down, Sandra. The nurse says you can see your father in a little while.'

'Thanks, Adèle, but I think I'll go out into the garden.'

She went to the French door and opened it. The fresh air

did her good. She walked out on the terrace, happy to be away from that crowded room which felt like an Egyptian tomb. Going down the five steps to the lawn, she took off her shoes to enjoy the sensation of the grass under her feet. It was wet with the cold night dew.

A solitary lantern lit the outbuildings. Sandra went towards the stables and slowly walked past them. They were empty, so the whinny she had heard when she arrived came from somewhere else. She remembered the stallion she had ridden at fifteen, and lost herself in happy memories of the past.

Then Adèle's voice calling her from the house brought her back to reality.

'Sandra, you can see him now. Come in!'

They went through the drawing room again and up the stairs, and found themselves outside the closed door.

Dr Blanchot was the first to come out.

'Good day, Sandra.' His voice was colourless, but his eyes showed his surprise at recognizing the woman before him as the girl who had once been his patient.

She hardly replied to his greeting. She opened the door just as another man, one she did not know, was coming out. He must be the cardiologist.

'Go in, mademoiselle, but don't tire him. He's very weak.'

The doctor seemed preoccupied. He stood back, holding the door open for Sandra, and she stepped into the room. Suddenly she felt apprehensive, as she had always done on those rare occasions when she was allowed into her parents' bedroom as a little girl. She saw the nurse, busy with some kind of apparatus on a trolley, and turned back to the man in the white coat.

'Does she really have to stay?'

'Yes, I'm afraid so, mademoiselle.'

But a voice rose from the big four-poster bed, a pretentious piece of furniture which Sandra's mother used to call her gondola. An enfeebled voice, but one that had lost none of its authority!

'Kindly leave us, mademoiselle!'

Its tone was firm. The nurse gave an indignant start and turned to the doctor, who signalled to her to obey. Shrugging her shoulders, the woman left the room.

Alone with her father, Sandra approached the bed. She saw that nothing had changed in Adrien's bedroom either. All traces of her mother's presence had been removed years ago, but she still could not help looking for the scent bottles on the dressing table, a negligee thrown over a chair.

Sandra began to tremble. As she came closer to the bed she saw a complicated piece of apparatus with wires and tubes running from it. Adrien had the needle of a drip feed stuck in his forearm. Several electrodes were attached to his chest with sticking-plaster. His pyjama jacket flapped around a body which seemed to have shrivelled up, like a plant no one has watered. Only the grey eyes were as bright as ever in the emaciated face. How old is he? Sandra suddenly wondered, and a nervous cough shook her as she thought how silly it was to ask such a question. Still, there *was* something ridiculous in the idea that she couldn't remember.

'Good day, Alexandra,' said Adrien.

'Hullo, Father.'

He hadn't called her Sandra, as he used to when she was a little girl. She wished her hands would stop shaking.

'Come and sit here beside me.'

She sat down on the bed, very carefully. He seemed so fragile she was afraid he would break at any sudden movement. Her eyes went to the green line tracing Adrien's heartbeat on a small screen. He caught her looking.

'Try to take no notice of those machines – they don't matter.'

Sandra cleared her throat. She felt as if her vocal cords were paralyzed, just as she did when she was a child and he wanted her to recite a piece of poetry to his friends.

Adrien took her hand and sat up a little way, with a grimace of pain.

'I didn't ask you to come here to talk about myself, Sandra.'

A faint light shone in his grey eyes, as if they wanted to absorb Sandra, draw her to him for the last time.

'We haven't seen each other since your marriage. I didn't want you to remember me only as I was then – you can't have a very favourable impression of me at that difficult time.'

He stopped, and swallowed. He was breathless, and each word was torture. Sandra thought she was observing these details with the detachment assumed by a medical student, but then she found her cheeks were wet. Adrien de Moncet did not seem to notice.

'My mistake,' he went on, 'was that I always thought of you as *my* daughter – only mine.'

His voice broke.

Sandra knew what those words must cost him. She pressed her father's hand.

'I always wanted to stifle anything in you that seemed to be inherited from your mother. I was wrong, and I'm paying for it. So are you.'

In sudden alarm, Sandra opened her mouth to speak, but the pressure of Adrien's thin fingers on hers stopped her.

'You don't have to make excuses for yourself. I bear just as much responsibility as you for what you are – what you have become.'

Sandra suddenly lowered her eyes. How did he know? Until now she had never asked herself if her father knew anything about it – about the Unicorn – or what he might think of it. Anyway, she was certain that her secrets would never leave the walls of the establishment. Perhaps she had even got a vague pleasure from the idea that he might find out some day? Well, now she knew that someone *had* told him. Who? Once again she tried to speak, but Adrien spoke first.

'I fought you, Sandra, and my own presentiments, and Marc – '

'Marc?'

'Yes. But I failed.'

Sudden intuition told Sandra that Adrien was not referring only to her marriage.

'Father, there's something I want to know,' she began in an urgent voice.

'It's not for me to tell you any more, Sandra. But I had to see you, to let you know . . . well, illness is a curious thing! It makes you want to wipe the slate clean, as if you'd never sinned, or let anyone down.'

Exhausted, de Moncet fell back on his pillows and closed his eyes.

Tears were streaming down Sandra's cheeks. Pictures came back to her from very far away. Pictures of tenderness and affection. For the first time she saw Adrien as a man who had suffered – had been wounded by a woman he loved and who had deserted him. And for the first time she felt guilty for bearing that woman's name.

'Off you go, my child. It's time you left. Be on your guard.'

He dismissed her with a last squeeze of her hand. She knew he was not strong enough to talk any more. She rose, still holding his hand in hers, bent and kissed him gently.

'I'll come back,' she said.

Eyes misted with tears, she left the room. The doctors and the nurse were already on their way back to the sick man's bedside.

13

The grey light of dawn broke over Route Nationale 306. Some minutes ago Sandra had realized that she ought to have taken the autoroute again.

She cast a worried glance in her mirror. The green Ford had been following her ever since she left Rambouillet. Without much hope, she stepped on the accelerator and passed the Dutch truck ahead of her. Then she pulled in, leaving as little space as possible between the truck and the BMW. She was cursing the melancholy mood which had led her to go back to Paris the longer way. She was in no hurry to get back there, to Marc and the Unicorn. She wanted time to think.

Now then, she told herself with a weary smile, find a way to get out of this one!

The angry Dutch driver flashed his lights at her. Unmoved, Sandra kept driving at the same speed. She did not have long to wait. The front of the Ford soon appeared in her wing mirror, and the green car drew level with the Dutch truck. Sandra saw a man at the wheel, but the pale light did not allow her to make out his features. Realizing what she had done, the stranger stayed in the left-hand lane, hooting at regular intervals. A Peugeot was coming up in the opposite direction. Doggedly, Sandra stayed close to the big truck. Still the Ford did not slow down. Its flashing lights expressed the driver's annoyance. Sandra awaited the inevitable accident.

At the last possible moment the Dutch truck braked, giving the Ford the room it needed to pull in. Sandra immediately accelerated. She was trying to increase the distance between herself and the American car. But the man did not seem to want to let her go.

They passed through Chevreuse. Sandra wondered whether to try throwing off her pursuer by turning into a minor road, going to Versailles and losing herself in its streets.

She hesitated. The traffic on the main road was good protection, even at this hour of the morning.

Suddenly exasperated by the grotesque situation, she slowed down. After all, who would really want to follow her, and why? She was beginning to feel the effects of fatigue, and of the tension of the last twenty-four hours. She guessed there was something that made sense of all that had happened, that it ought to add up to a clear answer in her mind. But the picture was hazy, and the car following her confused her even more.

The road was deserted ahead. A minor road turned off to the right, going through open fields where a few patches of hard snow clung in places. Sandra noticed this detail just as the Ford passed her. Had the man decided to give up, then?

A hundred metres or so ahead, the American car slewed across the road. Narrowing her eyes and fighting off panic, Sandra tried to assess her chances. All she could do was to turn up the minor road. The stranger realized what her intention was. He turned into it too, just a few seconds before the BMW.

The road was hardly more than a beaten track. Trying to avoid him, Sandra swung the wheel over to the right. Her car skidded, and slowly went into the ditch. With a pointless but instant reflex action, Sandra trod on the brake. She switched off the engine just as her head hit the side of the car door. Then there was silence.

She got out of her seat, managed to open the door, and found herself out on the road. Dazed, she put her hand to her forehead. Only a bump.

She raised her eyes and looked round her. There was the Ford, a little way off. A man was walking towards her. His breath rose in white spirals in the cold morning air.

'Sandra – are you all right?'

Marc placed his hand on her arm. Then he tried to put an arm round her shoulders. The fear she saw in his green eyes seemed to be genuine.

'Have you gone absolutely mad?' she asked, shaking him off. She sat down on the wing of the BMW, pushed back her mass of red hair with both hands, and then closed her eyes. 'Are you mad?' she repeated.

'I was really scared when I saw you go off the road. I thought the car might go up in flames.'

Slowly, Sandra opened her eyes. Her narrowed pupils looked beyond Marc, at the fallow field where three crows were scratching at the earth with their hard beaks. Suddenly one of the birds flew up with a harsh cry, passed overhead, and disappeared into the swirling mist.

'Why were you following me?'

He sat down beside her and put his hands in his trenchcoat pockets. Sandra shivered, hands clutching her shoulders, looking straight ahead of her.

'I missed you by just a few minutes at Rambouillet. Laure told me about it as soon as I arrived at the Rue des Licornes.'

Marc took his hands out of his pockets and turned up the collar of the trenchcoat.

'So of course you wanted to join me straight away?' she said, turning to face him.

Marc jumped nervously. 'Well, yes – of course.' He gazed at her in silence for a moment. She looked very fragile, shivering in her olive doeskin suit. 'Sandra, don't you have a coat?' he asked. 'You'll catch cold – here, come into my car.'

He offered her his arm. She recoiled, and abruptly stood up. On a screen, she seemed to see two naked bodies intertwined in lascivious pleasure.

She took a few steps along the road, kicking a clod of earth with the toe of her boot. He *may* be telling the truth, she thought. No, it comes too pat, her instinct told her, it's just too unbelievably solicitous. He had risen and was now walking beside her. Looking at the ground, he asked, 'How is your father?' Then, looking like a naughty child caught red-handed, he added, 'I mean, you haven't mentioned him yet.'

Sandra took a deep breath. Over in the field, the two remaining crows were quarrelling over a blackened ear of maize hardened by the cold.

'He's very ill,' she said. 'Though I doubt if you're really interested.' She was trying to catch his eye now; she wanted to sound him out. 'Why did you want to go acting like a gangster?'

He rubbed the back of his neck, and replied, with a contrite smile, 'Forgive me, Sandra. I wasn't really thinking. You're right, it *was* rather ridiculous.' She noticed that one of his eyelids had a nervous tic. 'Listen,' he went on, 'don't let's stay here. I'll send a breakdown truck for the BMW. Let's get back to Paris.'

Once again, he tried to approach her, but she would not take his arm and walked towards the Ford on her own. Her hand on the car door, she asked, 'Why a hired car? What happened to the Rover?'

'I – it had to go to the garage,' he said quickly, before getting behind the wheel.

Sandra too got in. As the Ford started, she watched the last wisps of mist disperse. The rising sun changed the iridescent air from yellow to blue. The two crows flew away from the bleak field together.

Back on the main road, Sandra kept her gaze on the asphalt. There was a sullen, dumb hostility between herself and Marc. She could tell he was looking furtively at her. He seemed to be waiting for something. For a good moment.

'What do the doctors say?'

She jumped, as if she had forgotten he was there.

'What doctors?'

'The doctors treating your father, Sandra.'

'I don't know. But I'm going back to see him tomorrow.'

She saw, quite clearly, how Marc compressed his lips.

She found a cigarette in her bag, and was irritated not to have a light. Marc offered her his lighter. Its flame sprang up too far, making beads of perspiration break out on her forehead.

'You haven't made things up with your father, have you?' he asked with a sarcastic smile.

He looked away from the road for a few seconds, something like contempt in his eyes as they rested on Sandra.

'I think I was as much in the wrong as he was. And our marriage – '

'Was a blow to him. I know – poor Adrien! Do *you* regret it?'

She said nothing.

'I get an impression your dear father has been telling you things which aren't much to my credit,' he said.

'Why should you think that?' she asked, rather too rapidly. To hide her alarm, she inhaled deeply as she smoked.

Marc waved an airy hand. He did not slacken speed when the Ford entered the Saint-Cloud tunnel. Eyes half-closed, Sandra listened to the noise of the vehicles driving through. The glaring lights lining the arch were projected intermittently on her eyelids. When they reached the embankment, Marc asked, 'Avenue Théophile-Gautier?'

'No, I'd rather go straight back to the Unicorn.'

'It would be more convenient for me to go to the apartment first. I have to pick up a file there.'

'Then drop me at a taxi rank,' was all she said.

He passed the broadcasting centre and turned right on the Pont Bir-Hakeim.

'Sandra, let's stop playing this little game,' he murmured, suddenly becoming tender. 'All this fuss because I didn't want you to face your father's illness alone! I realize I shouldn't have followed you the way I did, but I didn't know how else to catch up with you. I . . . '

'Marc, I'm worn out. We'll make our apologies to each other later, all right?'

Marc's hands had tightened on the steering wheel. Sandra saw his white, prominent knuckles. Suddenly, she badly wanted to get out of the car.

'I hope you don't mind,' she added slowly. 'I had quite a night of it.'

He smiled, and nodded. The Ford turned into the Avenue de Ségur, went along the Rue des Licornes, and stopped outside Number 6. Marc got out, came round the car and opened Sandra's door.

Laure came to meet them in the hall.

'Everything all right?' she asked, concern in her voice.

Sandra nodded.

'There's something I ought to tell you . . . '

'Later, Laure,' Sandra interrupted. She walked to the bottom of the stairs, turned and faced the other two. 'Just now I want a few hours' sleep.'

'I'll come up with you, Sandra,' said Marc. 'To tuck you in.'

He gave a harsh little laugh.

Sandra bit her lip, swallowed the sharp remark she had been about to make, and ran upstairs. Outside her bedroom door she made a last attempt.

'Thank you, Marc, but I can get to bed on my own.'

'I'd rather make sure of that,' he said with a charming smile.

He opened the door and stood aside for Sandra. She sighed briefly, and entered, her step hesitant. Tossing her bag on the bed, she looked for a cigarette in the box on the pedestal table, saw that it was empty, and stood there, her fingers interlocked. Marc came over to her. She felt the palms of his hands on her back, his breath on the nape of her neck.

'Sandra,' he murmured, kissing her ear.

His fingers gripped her slender waist, went up to her breasts, trapped beneath black cashmere. She freed herself with a movement of her shoulders.

'I need a cigarette.'

She went through the glazed double doors into her office, looking back. Marc's face gave nothing away, but she read such naked desire in his eyes that she began to tremble. In an instant, he caught up with her, pinning her against the edge of the desk. He took her face between his hands, stroking her neck. She felt his penis harden against her. Suddenly, he fastened his mouth on hers. She uttered a muffled little cry and tried to break away.

'No, Marc, not now. I can't!'

She tried to push him off, but he bent her back, forcing her to lie over the wooden desk top. Abruptly, he lifted her skirt and parted her legs. She twisted her head from left to right, trying to free her shoulders, but he was holding them firmly down on the desk.

'Marc, no! No! Stop it!'

But he was not listening. He had already undone his trousers, and now he was bundling up Sandra's skirt, exposing the black suspender belt that held her stockings up. He tore away her fine lace panties with his forefinger.

'Marc, please,' she gasped, making one last effort.

Jaw set, he looked at her uncomprehendingly. 'But you're mine, Sandra,' he said in a childlike voice. 'Mine!'

'No – not like this. Not like this!' she cried, as he was about to penetrate her.

'Monsieur Renan, I rather think your wife is speaking to you.'

It was a deep voice with a trace of American accent.

The high-backed red leather armchair behind the desk slowly swivelled round to face them.

'I really am so very sorry to interrupt this touching scene of conjugal bliss,' said Colonel Anderson.

14

Some moments seem to go on for ever. Shocked and humiliated, Sandra finally got the man before her into focus. She saw his tall figure, his reddish-blond beard, the scarred cheek, the eyes, which now looked black and not blue. Did the colonel wear coloured contact lenses? He was paler, too, without the make-up which had given him the high-coloured complexion of a drinking man. He looked altogether younger. She felt a dull ache inside her.

'What are you doing here? Who let you in?' Marc's voice was harsh, but the trembling of his hands as he re-adjusted his clothes showed how uneasy he was.

'One question at a time, my dear Renan.'

Colonel Anderson's grave voice was full of contempt. He walked round the desk and took a cigarette out of a black leather case. 'What am I doing here? Well, that shouldn't be too much of a mystery to you, should it?' He took a Zeppo lighter from his pocket and lit the cigarette. 'As for how I got in – well, all you need to do is book an appointment to get into this place, isn't that so?'

He gave a brief bark of laughter.

'Get out of here, Colonel Anderson!'

Marc had pulled himself together. He pointed a peremptory finger at the door.

Anderson inhaled deeply. 'You know my name? Well, isn't that odd! Of course, a unicorn is not the kind of animal to be satisfied with just one mistress.'

'What are you insinuating?'

Marc had gone pale. A vein was throbbing at his temple.

'However, it's only fair you should know my name, as *I* am well acquainted with *yours*,' Anderson went on imperturbably.

'Colonel, I am asking you for the last time to leave this room!'

Anderson crushed his cigarette out in the ash tray on the desk. 'That will do, Marc.' His impassivity seemed to have deserted him suddenly. 'There's no point playing this game any more.'

'I really don't see what – '

'Oh, stop it!' Sandra had cried out the words, and both heads turned towards her. The dark pair of eyes and the green ones both showed disquiet. She stepped forward, staggered, and clung to the back of the chair. Tears had left two dark tracks on her cheeks. She was standing in front of Anderson.

Her hands rose to the colonel's face, and her finger traced the scar across his cheek to his mouth, seeming to caress that strip of dead flesh. She took a long time over it: long enough for their eyes to meet and hold. Long enough for Marc, fists clenched, to lose his temper.

At last she said, 'James,' and dropped into an armchair, sobbing.

Marc said nothing. Sandra went on weeping, sick at heart to think she could have made love to this man, and her body and all her senses had not sent her a signal of recognition. Just like a machine.

Becoming James Llewelyn again, Anderson came over to her, gently took her hand, raised her chin and made her look at him.

'Sandra, I must explain . . . there's a lot I have to say to you.'

Suddenly rousing himself, Marc lunged at the other man, pushing him violently aside.

'Leave her alone! You can see you're upsetting her! Get out – now!'

'Not before I tell her about that night in Juan-les-Pins, and our bargain.'

Jaw set, Marc glared at James, and then lowered his eyes.

'Bargain?'

Sandra sat up in her chair. All this emotion and confusion suddenly brought an authoritative reflex into play. She was no longer crying as she said, looking sternly at the two men, 'Very well. I want to hear about it. *All* about it!'

Marc was looking like a waxwork. Hands behind his back, James took a few steps into the room, and then came back to face Sandra.

'So you shall.' His voice was gentle. 'That's why I've come back.' He glanced briefly at Marc, and then went on, 'We'll have to go back to our first meeting, Sandra.' He fell silent again, and then added, as if afraid of what was about to come, 'You'd better be prepared for a surprise.'

'Really?' said Sandra, with a wry smile.

James cleared his throat. 'I was at Rambouillet that day because your father and I were working togather on a matter which both our governments thought important.' He turned abruptly to Marc. 'I imagine your husband must have explained to you how diplomacy can lead to the service of the state in a less orthodox manner?'

Sandra avoided his eyes.

'This particular matter concerned a Romanian defector. A man called Smetlenko, who worked at the Soviet Embassy in Bucharest.'

Sandra gave a start. Smetlenko. She saw herself, six years earlier, shut in the closet next to Adrien's study and surrounded by papers and cobwebs.

'Along with Marc, who was working for your father, I was given the job of meeting the man. The two of us were to debrief him. To ensure his own safety, Smetlenko had made contact with both the French and the Americans. He claimed he could give us vital information about the activities of the Soviet Union in Angola and Vietnam, as well as other strategic points.'

James stopped and looked at Sandra.

'What has all this got to do with me?' She sounded irritated. She was watching Marc out of the corner of her eye – he was consulting his watch at frequent intervals, and kept looking at the door. To her mind, he was not quite as much like a rabbit in a trap as he should have been, and it bothered her.

'I'm coming to that,' said James. He sighed, as if he did not want to go on. 'No doubt you never thought much about the coincidence which brought us together on your uncle's yacht the day after you arrived in Juan-les-Pins, did you? It was all arranged.'

At this moment Marc stepped forward and crouched down in front of Sandra, who had seated herself again. He took her hands in his and pressed them, a little too hard.

'Sandra, look at me!' His voice was tense, almost imploring. 'Don't listen to him! None of what he's going to tell you is true, Sandra!'

He shook her hands as he spoke. She wanted to pull away from him, but she didn't dare.

'This place – we've built it up together,' Marc went on. 'Never forget that! I love you, Sandra! Come away from here. Let's leave him, let's go – now. There's still time.'

She suddenly saw something in his eyes she had never seen there before. Humility. Dependence. Slowly, she freed herself, rose, and walked round the desk.

'I must know, Marc.'

James said, very fast, as if he were afraid she might yield to Marc's next interruption, 'It was your uncle who got the defector away from Romania to France.'

She turned towards him, her eyes wide, her mouth open in an indignant exclamation. He did not give her time to speak.

'Men like Gregory are very valuable to the secret services. They like taking risks for their own sake. Smetlenko was on board the *Rosebud* that evening. On the well-tried principle of the stolen letter, he was mingling with the guests. You even danced with him yourself.'

Sandra put a hand to her mouth. The fat man who had been drinking and trod on her toes! And May – yes, of course, May was in it too. Sandra suddenly realized just what had been going on around her, naive as she was.

'Go on,' she said harshly.

James looked away and mechanically stroked his beard. He suddenly seemed unhappy, and his voice was not as confident as before when he went on, 'What happened next – well, it hadn't been planned. You must believe me, Sandra! We were both in love with you.'

His eyes clung to hers, as if to impart his message to the violet of their irises.

Sandra turned to Marc. By now he did indeed look like a trapped animal. He was casting furtive glances at the door. Oddly enough, she found that reassuring. James did not seem interested in Marc's behaviour. She decided she believed him.

'We were sincere that night, Sandra. But there was already a shadow between us.'

'The rest of the story's for me to tell, if you don't mind,' said Marc. He wore a mocking smile now. 'Because there's a sequel, my dear Sandra – or rather, a prelude. And if I'm to lose you – ' he stopped, and took a long look at both of them – 'I'd rather you heard it from me. The Unicorn was a project that had been planned before I ever met you. In fact, it was my own brainchild, and I got my superiors to adopt it. There was only one problem: finding the right woman. We needed someone really exceptional to run the place. As soon as I saw you, I knew you would be the woman I was looking for. All I had to do was train you for the job.'

Marc's eyes shone with a strange glow, as if he were reliving those moments and enjoying them all over again. His hands gestured nervously, miming his enthusiasm. He came over to Sandra, who stepped back in alarm.

'So my bosses gave the go-ahead,' he went on. 'Everything was ready. But your uncle got wind of our plans, and told James – no doubt because he couldn't or didn't want to approach your father. Poor Adrien. It would have killed him.' Marc's mouth twisted as he placed himself in front of his rival. 'Well – this knight errant of yours tried to oppose my plans!'

James looked him up and down with dislike. Indeed, he seemed to be having difficulty in not going for Marc's throat.

'Look at him! Even now he's itching to get at me – and we almost came to blows at the time.' He swung round and turned to Sandra. 'Marc Renan and James Llewelyn fighting over you – what do you say to that, my lovely? Luckily, I was covered by my bosses. He couldn't try anything on without exposing Smetlenko to risk. And as his own bosses wanted the Romanian at any price, he was caught in a trap.'

Marc dropped into an armchair. The laugh he gave was harsh, almost a sob. His head fell on his breast, and when he raised it he seemed almost sad.

'So I suggested doing a deal.'

Sandra tried to speak, but her throat was constricted. For some hours, she had been feeling like a punch-drunk boxer intent on nothing but trying to keep his feet.

'I accepted it, Sandra,' said James, with difficulty. 'My superiors wanted to get the Romanian away from the French. And the bargain was worth nothing after all. I've had six years to regret it.'

He stopped, looked for a cigarette, and turned away from Sandra.

'The deal was that he would let me leave that night, taking Smetlenko with me, if I promised never to come into your life again.'

There was a long silence. The magic circle was broken: his mere stating the terms of the bargain had done it. Only the outcome remained to be told.

Voice weary, James went on, 'Later, we found out that Smetlenko was only a minor civil servant, making out he was someone important. He knew no more about the secret files than we ourselves did already! And I'm still wondering how Marc knew *that* . . . '

The door screeched on its hinges as a man kicked it open and came in. A man of forty who looked like a businessman, greying at the temples, in an elegant overcoat.

'Looks as if I'm just in time,' said Mallowan cheerfully.

15

Sandra knew he was Marc's right-hand man, but until now she had chosen to forget his existence. She had wanted to forbid him access to the Unicorn, and Marc had respected her wishes. The mere sight of Mallowan made her shudder, reminding her of their humiliating encounter under the archway of a Parisian apartment building's entrance, and her imprisonment in the Café Américain. Just now he was the last person in the world she would have wished to see again.

'Mallowan! At last!' Marc was breathing hard, like a runner after a race. 'I thought you'd never arrive!'

'You said eleven-thirty, M. Renan,' said the man.

Leaning in the doorway, he tipped his hat back. He looked like a cat cautiously sizing up the situation before venturing into the room.

Sandra knew he was dangerous, and for a split second she wondered if James knew too. The American did not seem surprised, merely annoyed.

A sign from Marc was enough for Mallowan. He was used to obeying without question, ready to go into action like a well-oiled machine when the word was given.

Sandra did not see it coming. By the time she realized what was happening, he was already on her. He put a hand over her mouth, twisted one arm behind her back, and dragged her out to the landing. James sprang after her, but Marc moved first, blocking his way.

'Keep still, and she won't be hurt.'

Sandra struggled; she wanted to shout. She tried in vain to bite the hand gagging her. James hesitated.

'You wouldn't dare,' he said, a challenge in his voice.

'Maybe not – but Mallowan wouldn't hesitate,' said

Marc.

Llewelyn sighed. His hands dropped to his sides.

'Get back to the desk,' Marc told him.

James took three steps backwards. He looked at Sandra, who was struggling and kicking in Mallowan's powerful grasp. He would not admit himself defeated.

'Don't worry, Sandra. We'll soon meet again.'

'I wouldn't count on it! said Marc, before closing the office door and turning the key in the lock.

Mallowan was already on his way downstairs with his captive. Marc joined them on the next landing. The Unicorn was still asleep at this time of day, apart from the domestic staff in the kitchens. He was almost certain to be able to leave the house unnoticed.

But as they started over the marble flags paving the hall, a voice came from the drawing room. 'Is that you, Sandra?'

Laure's shape was framed in the doorway. She felt rather than understood that something was wrong.

'What's going on?' she cried. 'Marc!'

Taking advantage of her friend's presence, Sandra tried to break free again, but her abductor had a firm hold on her. Marc was about to say something when Laure flung herself at Mallowan.

'Let her go!'

He pushed her away with his free hand, flinging her against the banisters. Laure's head hit the hard wood. Slowly, she collapsed on the floor, without a sound.

'You're mad!' Marc whispered. 'You may have killed her!'

'Do you want to get out of here, or not?'

Marc looked at the crumpled body lying on the white marble. He hesitated for just a moment, and then joined Mallowan, who had already crossed the courtyard.

The Ford was still standing outside. Marc opened the back door of the car, and Mallowan pushed Sandra into the black-upholstered seat. She shrank away, and tried to open the other door. Marc got in beside her.

'You drive,' he told Mallowan. 'No use breaking your nails,' he said to Sandra. 'You can see it's locked.'

She stiffened, darting a hostile look at him, and then sat back against the side of the car, as far as possible from her husband.

The Ford set off. 'Where to?' asked Mallowan.

'The meeting place.'

Marc's face was hard again. He seemed to have forgotten about Sandra, and was looking straight ahead.

'That's dangerous now. Much too dangerous,' said Mallowan, without turning round. 'Suicidal!'

'Don't argue. We have no choice.'

Sandra closed her eyes, unable to stand the sound of her own heart beating.

James had not wasted time trying to break the door down; he merely went round through Sandra's bedroom and found himself out on the landing.

He ran downstairs and came upon Laure's unconscious body. Quickly, he bent and put a hand to her throat. The jugular vein was beating steadily against his palm. He lifted Laure and carried her into the drawing room, and then went to the domestic quarters to tell the staff.

The Ford stopped outside Number 14, Avenue Théophile-Gautier. Marc put a hand on the car door handle.

'You wait here – I won't be long.'

'What about her?' asked Mallowan.

Marc glanced at Sandra. Sitting in the corner, face impassive, she looked like a wrathful goddess.

'She comes with us. I'll see to it. Everything will be all right.'

He closed the car door behind him and went into the apartment building through its glazed door.

A few moments later he came back, carrying a small, black leather travelling bag.

'Let's go. We'll be late,' he said, getting into the car again.

'Where *are* we going?' Sandra suddenly asked.

Marc seemed to be exhausted. 'Don't worry. I just have a little business to settle before leaving Paris. I didn't think I'd have to take steps of this kind quite so soon, but the sudden appearance of your friend James means I've had to put my plans forward.'

'I'm not interested in your plans, Marc.

'Don't forget we're husband and wife, for better or worse.'

'I don't want to go with you,' she shouted. 'I don't want to leave France – that's your idea, isn't it?'

'You have no choice.'

The Ford began moving again.

James had handed Laure over to the little Arab maid, who went to wake one of the girls. He found the telephone in the drawing room, called a Rambouillet number, and spoke to someone at the other end of the line for several minutes. Then he dialled again: a radio telephone number.

'Where are they now?' he asked.

'Still in the Ford. On the embankment.'

'Don't lose sight of them. I'll join you at Charenton.'

'Right.'

They were driving towards Bercy. Sandra was sitting back again, silent, trying to put her ideas into order.

'*Why* are you taking me with you?' she suddenly asked. 'Do you really think I can ever look at you again without disgust? As if I hadn't been through enough these last few hours!'

He sounded like a thwarted child as he replied, 'Sandra, I've betrayed my country for you. I'm not letting you escape me now.'

She told herself that was not the way to tackle him. He was beyond reason.

'You wriggled out of it pretty well, for a traitor,' she said harshly.

He turned to her. Her face was icy.

'Why? Because I managed to make them believe James

had tricked me? Because, as I'd guessed, Smetlenko turned out to be only a miserable little functionary of no interest to anyone? I'd still deliberately let what could have been an important source of information for us get away.'

'I betrayed my country,' he repeated, as if it gave him some strange kind of pleasure. 'And I'll do it again.'

'Those cassettes!'

Suddenly Sandra realized the full significance of his flight.

An ironic little smile hovered on Marc's lips.

'I know what you're going to do, Marc. I saw you recording a copy of the videotape last night.'

His smile grew wider. 'I thought I heard a sound!'

Facing this imperturbable man who was still trying to pretend he had made use of her out of love, Sandra felt nothing but anger.

'From the very beginning – ' she started, but her anger choked her.

He was looking straight ahead again.

'Everything you suspect is true, Sandra. There's no point in hiding it from you now. The information picked up at the Unicorn doesn't go just to the French government. I've sold the stuff all over the place – to all sorts of people! Some of those films have gone to connoisseurs of pornography, and for very good money too!'

'You knew James would come back some day, didn't you?'

She had passed from anger to despair. Twice, now, she had let herself be hoodwinked and dragged into a game which was none of her choosing.

'Yes, of course,' he said, as calm as ever. 'So I took all the necessary precautions. I recognized him as soon as he turned up disguised as Colonel Andersen. It took *you* rather longer, didn't it?'

She turned her head away, biting her lip to keep from crying.

'There's a Bentley behind us,' Mallowan remarked.

'Perhaps James has taken precautions of his own,' murmured Sandra, pleased to see alarm re-born on Marc's face.

'Step on it!' he said.

James was back on the southern Périphérique. He saw the Bentley when he reached the Charenton slip road. As they had agreed, the big English car fell behind, and Llewelyn's Renault took over, going towards Joigny. There were no traffic jams at this time in the early afternoon. James lifted the radio telephone.

'Got them,' he said. 'See you at the Rue de Paris.'

'It's gone,' said Mallowan.

Marc leaned back in his seat as the Ford turned into the Rue de Paris. A little farther on the car went up a slope before stopping on a bend, outside a tall doorway of worm-eaten wood. One side of the double door was open. Mallowan got out to open the other, and then drove the car into a small, stone-paved courtyard overgrown with weeds. A high wall separated the property from the street. They were facing an old stone house with two assymetrical wings. Several window panes were broken and the shutters, their paint flaking, hung off their hinges. The glazed front door was open.

Mallowan was first out of the car, followed by the other two.

'You go in,' Marc told him. 'Tell him we've got what he wants, and we can't wait.'

Mallowan went into the house. Through the open door, Sandra saw an empty hall with a bleached floor, leading to another room, of which she could see nothing but the window.

Three minutes later Mallowan came back.

'Okay. But he says you must leave at once.'

'I was afraid of that.'

'And he says it won't be easy. They've noticed the leaks at NATO, and the Americans are on the trail.'

'I know.' Marc cut him short with a gesture. He picked

up the black leather case, and then, holding Sandra firmly by the arm, went up the five steps to the door and entered the hall. Mallowan followed them.

They entered a big, unfurnished room. Here, too, the floor seemed to have been washed with bleach. White plaster was crumbling from the walls, and two rusty garden chairs stood in the middle of what had once been a drawing room. A man in a dark suit stood by one of the three French doors which opened on to the slope of a garden.

James had left his car at the bottom of the slope. He knew that the Bentley and a van had taken up positions round the bend at the top of the hill. A third vehicle was now going round the block to station itself outside the gate at the end of the garden.

James went through the tall doorway and got into the cover of a tree. Then he made a signal. Shadowy figures began to move cautiously forward behind him. James approached the steps, going carefully from tree to tree. He did not want to be spotted yet.

Without turning round, the man began to speak. 'Your last deliveries were much appreciated, but now we must call a halt. I am afraid you may have become too conspicuous. A pity.'

'I'm afraid of that, too.'

Marc was looking for something in the case. He produced a carefully packaged little parcel. The cassettes, thought Sandra, repressing a shudder. The last delivery – and mine is sure to be among them! She could not help feeling there was something entirely expected about this scene, and though she was uneasy she was surprised to find she did not feel afraid.

'I didn't expect the woman.'

'She goes with me,' said Marc firmly.

'It will be difficult to get two of you out.'

'She goes with me.'

At last the man turned towards them. His face was the [illegible]d it is easy to forget.

'Very well. I'll leave you now.' He gave Marc a brown envelope, and took the package. 'You'll find your instructions in there. Follow them to the letter, and you'll be out of France this evening.'

Then he turned to Mallowan, who had remained in the background.

'What about you?'

'No, thank you. I don't like travelling! I shall disappear in my own way.'

James had been waiting in the hall for several minutes. He was looking at his watch, as if waiting for a signal.

Without another word, the man turned his back on Sandra and Marc, opened one of the French doors and walked out into the garden.

Violently, James kicked the door open.

'You're surrounded. No use running for it!'

At that moment, five men in black burst through the other three doors into the room. They surrounded Marc and Sandra. Mallowan had already dashed out of the French door, following the man in the dark suit, who was running for the gate at the far end of the garden.

'I wouldn't advise you to follow their example,' said James, when he saw Marc move towards the French doors, dragging Sandra with him. 'There are men waiting at the gate.'

Slowly, the six men approached Marc. Looking tense and haggard, he slipped a hand into his coat – and it was that moment that Sandra chose to tear herself away. With a violent movement, she made him let go of her and took refuge in James's arms.

'I told you we'd see each other again soon,' he murmured.

Marc's hand fell by his side as the five men seized him.

Heavy footsteps sounded in the hall, and a man with silvery hair entered the room twirling a silver-topped cane.

'They've got the other two,' said Gregory Aladin. 'This time, my dear nephew by marriage, your game is well and truly up.'

16

The Lear Jet was flying over Clermont-Ferrand, but its passengers were not much interested in the landscape below. In the little grey saloon, the steward placed two Manhattans on the round table, and went out. Sandra waited for him to close the sliding door after him. Then she leaned over and picked up one of the cocktails. James raised his own glass.

'To victory?'

His smile showed sharp white teeth.

She moistened her lips with the amber liquid, a misty look in her eyes.

'Maybe.'

She leaned back in her seat, closing her eyes.

'It's all happened too fast. I feel as if I'd lost a day of my life.'

'I wish I could have spared you all that,' he said. 'But it just wasn't possible.'

She opened her eyes again and looked at him, trying to recapture an image from the past. He had found the time to shave his beard and moustache. All that was left of Colonel Andersen was the bleached fair hair. That and the scar. Llewelyn looked more like her memory of him now. At first she had thought the scar was a fake; now she couldn't take her eyes off it, as if that pale mark were the proof of their separation.

'That scar,' she began. 'I don't even know where you got it!'

He put his glass down, leaned forward and clasped his hands on his knees. 'In Vietnam.'

She said nothing, waiting for him to fill in the gap of years between them of his own accord.

'I was sent there on a mission. I could have refused, but I didn't.'

He stopped, and looked through the porthole at the white wing of the aircraft, shining in the sun.

'Why?'

'I wanted to forget. I thought war would cure me. But as you see, I was wrong.'

He said no more.

'And then?'

'Then?' He straightened up. 'Oh, I went on living, went on working for the government – both officially and unofficially. I stopped trying to forget. I was always thinking of you. And Marc.'

There was an awkward silence between them. Sandra drunk half her cocktail in one gulp.

'How did you find out the truth about Marc?'

He seemed relieved by the change of subject. 'I'd kept in touch with Gregory and May. Through them, I always knew where you were, and I could follow your husband's activities pretty closely. I was biding my time.'

She lowered her eyes. 'I did try to trace you.'

'I know. And I know what that cost you. I was already suspecting Marc by then. I thought he'd make a mistake some day. They all do. Marc had incredible luck in having the trust of his government. It took a series of leaks from NATO before we could do anything.'

'NATO? What's NATO got to do with all this?'

He smiled, and explained patiently. 'The countries of the North Atlantic Treaty Organization share certain secrets which they do *not* like to see put on public display. As long as information reaches only allies like France who are trying to keep up to date, well, that's not so bad. We knew exactly what was going on at the Unicorn. We left it alone. But then we noticed that information passing through Paris turned up in East Berlin, Warsaw, Moscow – and it was time for my Service to step in.'

'You might have suspected me, too.'

He shook his head. 'No, right from the start you were out of your depth. Marc made use of you in a revolting way.'

'Yes, I suppose so.'

'Sandra . . . '

She knew what he was going to say, but she was not ready to listen yet, and told him so with her eyes.

'What are you going to do with Marc?' she asked, suddenly on the verge of tears. 'And me? Why am I here?'

His soft laugh was soothing. 'Take it easy! Not so many questions all at once.'

'I really do need to know, James.'

'I didn't want to give this mission too much of an official character. That's why I asked Gregory to help me.'

'You're not going to let Marc go?'

'He was more than a friend to me, you know – almost a brother. My Service doesn't require a culprit. Especially not if he turns out to be a French diplomat who was also working for his own country's secret services. All we need is to be sure that no more leaks occur. And after all, I've got Mallowan and the contact, if someone really *has* to be produced.'

'So what's the idea of this journey?'

You forget that Marc and I did a deal. What has been done must be undone.'

The door of the little saloon suddenly opened.

'I have an idea you're discussing me.'

Marc's smile was ironic. He looked at them for a long time, and then stepped backwards.

'I just came to say we're about to land. Yes, that's what I was going to tell you,' he murmured, before he closed the sliding door again.

The jet came down on a private airfield not far from Juan-les-Pins. Four passengers got out, and went straight to a large black limousine. The car followed the coastal road, passed Juan itself, and stopped outside a villa which Sandra recognized at once. It was the one that belonged to Annabelle, the girl on the yacht. James saw her look, and explained, 'Annabelle's a friend of Gregory's.'

The villa was empty. The drawing room, with its white walls, had seemed pleasantly cool that summer, but was chilly with oblivion today.

However, Sandra had forgotten nothing. She knew something important was going to happen. They were all four there, three judges and one accused. To reassure herself, she sought Gregory's glance. He smiled, came over and took her by the shoulders.

'Gregory, I do so wish it could all be different!' she said, leaning against his strong chest.

'Come on, Tsarina, you're not going to flinch now, are you?'

Gently, he disengaged himself. 'I'll leave you now,' he added. 'I won't be far away. I must let your father know that everything's all right.'

'Adrien knew right from the start, didn't he?'

'No, not from the start,' said James. 'I only went to him for help and advice a few months ago – once I'd found out the origin of those leaks for certain.'

'Why don't we finish all this?' Marc suddenly spat. 'You're going to have plenty of time to explain things later.'

Leaning against the fireplace, he was nervously stroking his thigh. Three heads turned to look at him.

'Why did you bring me here? What do you want from me?'

Gregory pressed Sandra's hand and disappeared into another room. James pulled out a chair for Sandra. He himself remained standing.

'I'm going to suggest we do another deal, Marc.'

'Are you, indeed?'

'You're finished, and you know it. But for the sake of our past friendship I'd rather not hand you over to the police.'

Marc turned abruptly to him. 'For Sandra's sake, more likely!'

'Yes, that's so. I haven't forgotten she bears your name.'

'My poor dear James! You're somewhere up in the

clouds. You don't know what Sandra is – what she's become. The Unicorn . . . '

'The Unicorn is in the past!'

Sandra had risen, and was looking challengingly at Marc. He held her gaze for several seconds, and then turned away his head.

'I know what *you* made her,' said James harshly.

Marc made a gesture of irritation. 'Well, what's this deal of yours?'

James took a deep breath. 'I'll let you go free – on condition you never see Sandra again, and leave the country for good.'

Sandra felt the tension in her whole being. James seemed impassive. She realized that he was trying to ransom six years of shame for her.

Marc said nothing. He turned to the fireplace and put both his hands on the cold stone mantelpiece. He remained for several seconds, head bowed on his fingers.

'Well, you've won anyway,' he said. 'You've got what you wanted. As for what *I* wanted – ' He straightened up and turned to them. 'After all, I was going to leave the country in any case, so . . . '

'Is that your decision, Marc?'

'I suppose it might be nobler to choose prison, but I'll take your deal.'

'You'll leave tomorrow, then. Gregory will take you anywhere you want.'

'On one condition.'

'You really think you can make conditions?' James's tone had hardened.

Marc approached Sandra. She saw, in his eyes, that humility and total dependence which both fascinated and disgusted her. Even now, she could not decide if it was assumed, or if this was Marc's real face.

'Well, call it a favour,' he said. 'It's you I want to ask, Sandra.'

She shifted uneasily in her chair.

'Sandra, before I go, I want to make love to you one last time.'

17

The beach was deserted. The last glimmers of the twilight lay on the sand, grey, like the fine mist of spray on her face, like the slow waves of the leaden sea. Sandra was sitting under a pine, pretending not to have known her feet must bring her to this place.

She looked at the sea, trying to gather her thoughts. She couldn't manage to feel hatred for Marc – only disgust. Vengeance was too abstract an idea. Reparation and readjustment, those were the words that came to her mind. Undoing the past, putting her life back in order. That had begun yesterday – but she knew very well that her destiny had been fixed six years earlier, at the precise spot where she now sat. At the moment, it did not seem that time had been on her side. She had thought she could run faster than her memories.

A trickle of sand ran from her palm. Well, yet again she must do something if she was to survive. She rose and went back to the black car pulled into the side of the road. Now she knew what she had to do.

She found James and Marc where she had left them: seated face to face in the drawing room of the villa, watching each other. Her husband's last words still hung in the air, obscene in their simplicity, heavy with a long past history which was taking its time to die.

She faced them, her hair wet and windblown, her lips shining. She knew that at that moment they desired her with a force nothing could stop.

'I'll let you have your favour,' she said, directly. 'But *I* am making a condition too.'

She looked at each of them in turn – and felt good for the first time in two days.

'I'll make love to you, Marc,' she went on, '*and* to James.'

She read her triumph in Marc's face. Slowly, he nodded. Without a word, James watched her go to the room he had left six years before. As she went, she shed her clothes, dropping them on the floor.

At first they hesitated. Then they rose and followed her.

By the time she reached the bedroom she was naked.

They dared not approach, but stood in the doorway, waiting for a signal.

'You both love me, don't you?' she asked in a clear voice.

She saw the unmistakable answer in their eyes.

'Then show me!'

She came towards them, took their hands and led them to the bed.

Marc touched her first. His hands on her breasts were icy, but they slowly became warmer, sliding over Sandra's rounded buttocks. He tried to find her mouth, but she twisted away, looking at James.

'Undress,' she told Marc.

He straightened up and quickly removed his clothes. Sandra had gone over to James. She kissed him full on the mouth, clinging to him. She felt him tremble. He caressed her body slowly, almost reverently.

She could feel Marc's penis behind her, hard and impatient. He drew her against him and lay on the bed, dragging her down with him. In sudden frenzy, he kissed her breasts, sucking them greedily. Then his mouth came down to the blazing triangle of her hair and slid towards the warm, wet groove beneath it.

Sandra felt for James's hand.

'Oh yes, lick me! she said. 'Lick me there!'

Marc slid both hands under Sandra's buttocks, raised her pubis and put his face to it.

She drew James towards her. She wanted his penis in her mouth. She shivered when she felt the hot flesh between her lips.

Marc had straightened up. 'I want to take you, Sandra – let me take you.'

She moaned, her hips rising as if to summon him.

James's penis left her mouth just as Marc's entered her. She gasped with pleasure.

'Oh, make me come! Make me alive!'

Marc's body was on top of hers, their genitals intermingled, their hips clinging together as they followed the rhythm imposed on them by their desire.

'I love it!' cried Sandra. 'Oh, it's good – so good!'

And Marc lost control as if he wanted to wipe out everything else, leaving nothing but the trace of his body inside her.

She felt he was ready to come, and opened her eyes.

'No, wait. Not like that! Wait!'

He stopped, pain in his face, and looked uncomprehendingly at her.

'I want you both,' she said. She looked at James, whose hand she was still holding. 'Like the first time. Lie down.'

She drew away from Marc's embrace and pressed close to James. Then she sat astride him, slowly letting herself slip down on his erect penis. Her movements were harmonious and assured, chosen to enhance her own pleasure and his. Her breathing was hoarse. His eyes closed, James abandoned himself to her caresses. 'Oh, I want to come!' she cried.

James opened his eyes and smiled at her. 'You're beautiful!'

She leaned down to lie flat on him, embracing him, and her hips moved faster.

'Marc, take me – take me from behind!'

Resigned, he placed himself behind her, pressing close to her buttocks, and penetrated her with a single thrust of his penis.

She cried out, and then kept still for a moment, taking her pleasure from feeling their two penises reconciled inside her.

'Oh, fill me up!' she cried.

And slowly, they began to move, each wanting to possess

her. Sandra had closed her eyes. At that moment all the men in her life – forgotten, loved, rejected, remembered – were united in one double penis thrusting and plunging at her.

Her body arched. She gasped, searching for a mouth, a face, and found James's.

'Sandra, I love you!' cried Marc.

His body moved spasmodically against her back as he came.

James lay there taut, almost as if in pain. Hoarse breath escaped his lips, and then his features relaxed. He repeated Sandra's name over and over, like a litany.

She said nothing. She came, triumphantly.

Pale sunlight filled the room, tracing golden patterns on the walls. Sandra woke to feel an erect penis close to her.

'I was watching you sleep,' he said. 'It was beautiful. You looked like a child – lovely and terrifying.'

'Why?' she asked, clinging to him.

'Because you're *not* a child.'

Her trill of laughter was fresh and clear – liberated, perhaps, he thought as he crushed her in his arms.

Somewhere in the Mediterranean, she knew, the *Rosebud* was sailing east. On board, a solitary passenger watched the coast disappear from sight.